**ALSO BY MOLLY B. BURNHAM**

*TEDDY MARS BOOK #1:*
*Almost a World Record Breaker*

# TEDDY MARS
## ALMOST A WINNER

## MOLLY B. BURNHAM

Illustrations by
## TREVOR SPENCER

KATHERINE TEGEN BOOKS
An Imprint of HarperCollins Publishers

Katherine Tegen Books is an imprint of HarperCollins Publishers.

Teddy Mars Book #2: Almost a Winner
Text copyright © 2016 by Molly B. Burnham
Illustrations copyright © 2016 by Trevor Spencer

Library of Congress Cataloging-in-Publication Data
Burnham, Molly B.
    Almost a winner / Molly B. Burnham ; illustrations by Trevor Spencer. —
First edition.
        pages      cm. — (Teddy Mars ; 2)
    Summary: "When Teddy's whole class decides to break a bigger, better
world record, friends turn into enemies, and Teddy is forced to do something
he's never done before—try not to break a world record"— Provided by
publisher.
    ISBN 978-0-06-227813-5 (hardback)
    [1. World records—Fiction.   2. Family life—Fiction.   3. Schools—
Fiction.   4. Friendship—Fiction.   5. Humorous stories.]   I. Spencer, Trevor
(Artist), illustrator.   II. Title.
PZ7.B93515Al  2016                                          2015015670
[Fic]—dc23                                                        CIP
                                                                   AC

Typography by Erin Fitzsimmons
16  17  18  19  20   CG/RRDH   10 9 8 7 6 5 4 3 2 1

First Edition

To my folks, Mom, Pop, and Joanne.
You are my wisecracking, straight-talking,
hardworking, always-enthusiasticators. In other
words, my I'm-nothing-without-you-ators.

## GROSSER THAN GRAVY WRESTLING

The day my brother covered himself in pigeon poo and feathers was the day I knew my life would never be normal again. And that's saying something, because with five older sisters and a little brother I call The Destructor, normal is not possible.

I admit, I actually thought I had made peace with The Destructor. It seemed funny when I first found him covered in a layer of pigeon poo and feathers. And I even laughed when he said, "Call me Pigeon Boy!" and then cooed like a real pigeon. He is only five, after all. I figured, if pigeon poo is strong enough to stick the feathers onto his clothes, how worried should I be?

But then The Destructor hugged me.

Being hugged by a kid covered in pigeon poo and feathers is not funny. I know this because even though pigeon poo is very sticky, it's not sticky enough to stop it from smearing all over everything it touches.

By *everything* I do mean *me*.

Which explains why, at this very moment, just like The Destructor, I am covered in pigeon poo and feathers!

Strange but true, the only way I could be any grosser right now is if I were Joel Hicks, the guy who, according to *The Guinness Book of World Records*, holds the record for *most* wins at the World Gravy Wrestling Championships.

Seriously, wrestling in a pool of gravy!

To be perfectly honest, I'd rather wrestle in gravy

than be hugged by The Destructor. Even when he's not covered in poo. Unfortunately, I wasn't given a choice.

## THERE WILL ALWAYS BE MORE

Most people call my brother Jake. That's what my parents named him, but he'll always be The Destructor to me. Here is a list of reasons why I call him The Destructor. This list only includes what he's done this year. There isn't enough paper in the world to make a list for all five of his years.

1. Destroyed my Star Wars action figures: he ripped them apart with his bare hands.
2. Destroyed my birthday #1: he puked all over the place.
3. Destroyed my birthday #2: he passed his puking to everyone in my family.
4. Destroyed my birthday #3: he opened all my presents.
5. Destroyed my sneakers: he clogged the toilet with a sock and pee water overflowed all over my feet.
6. Destroyed my copy of *The Guinness Book of World Records*: he drew all over it.

7. Destroyed my tent: he jumped on it and skunked it.
8. Destroyed my world record: he thought I was in trouble because I was covered in pigeons, but I was trying to break the record for most pigeons on a person. It's true that I was in pain, but again, I was not in trouble.

## THERE WILL ALWAYS BE MORE PART 2

There are so many more things I could say about The Destructor. But what I have come to realize is that there will always be more destruction.

## MOM

Like usual, when I walk into the kitchen, Mom is reading her newspaper. She looks up at The Destructor and me, and then her glasses slide off her face and land on the floor. She doesn't try to stop them or even pick them up. "What world record were

you trying to break this time?"

"Mom," I say, "this is obviously not a record."

"Well," she says, finally reaching down for her glasses, "you never know."

She's right to wonder. Over the past year I have tried to break a lot of world records.

## SOME OF THE RECORDS I ALMOST BROKE

1. Pushing an orange the farthest with just my nose.
2. Stretching the most rubber bands across my face.
3. And, of course, getting the most pigeons to land on me.

## THE RECORD I BROKE

I am happy to say I do hold a world record now. I slept in a tent the longest time for anyone under the age of twelve. And I'm only ten! The next version of *The Guinness Book of World Records* will probably have my name and a picture of me in it. Or maybe I'll be on the website. I don't care which, because they are both amazing, and being in either will be the greatest moment of my life.

And strange but true, I have my family to thank for it, because they knew I was breaking a record when I didn't know it myself. I guess I also have The Destructor to thank, because he drove me out of the house and into the tent, but

I'll never admit that to him, because it's not like he was trying to help me. He was just being him. Honestly, sleeping in the tent was not so hard. At this very moment I am, in fact, wondering why I ever moved back into the house.

Clearly, it was a moment of weakness.

Anyway, my point is that under the circumstances, it's not surprising that Mom thinks I was trying to break a record.

Mom looks at The Destructor and me all covered in pigeon poo and feathers and sighs really deeply and then says, "It's not even bath night."

## BATH NIGHT VS. GROUP RECORDS

A couple of years ago, Dad decided one bath a week was fine for anyone under six. He also said that with nine people in our family, our water bill was high enough.

I know some people think taking a bath only once a week is gross, but if you lived with The Destructor you would agree with Dad, because no human can actually stand his screaming more than once a week.

The Destructor hates baths as much as I hate group records in *The Guinness Book of World Records*. Those are the records where a bunch of people do the exact same thing at the exact same time. For example, there's a record for the most people brushing their teeth together (13,380) or, the alway-gross most people hugging (5,369). (Yuck!)

I admit, the largest snowball fight (5,834 people) and the largest pillow fight (4,201 people) sound fun, but still, breaking a record should require more than just a lot of people doing the same thing at once. I mean, that's just fun. And I don't think breaking a record should ever just be fun. Breaking a record should definitely involve hardship and suffering.

Which is basically what I'm going through right now. I thought maybe The Destructor would change his mind about baths once he became Pigeon Boy. Pigeons are very clean birds and take baths every day.

But The Destructor has not changed. Even with two pillows covering each ear and tied onto my head with an old scarf, I can hear him howling all the way from the upstairs bathroom.

I can't hear anything Mom says until she hollers, "Jake! Get back in the bathtub this minute!" And two seconds later The Destructor streaks past me, yelling, "Whatever you do, don't tell

Mom where I'm hiding!" He dives under the sofa.

This just seems to prove my point about group records and The Destructor's feelings about baths.

We both want to stay as far away from them as possible.

## MOM'S TO-DO LIST

Mom keeps a list of everything she needs to do in a day. She calls it her *to-do list*. I like these lists. They are orderly in a way that my family is not. There's something cool about how she adds things to it and crosses things off. She sometimes also loses her list and tries to remember what was on it. This does not usually go so well.

I remember one time Mom lost her list and forgot to do laundry, and I had to wear a pair of pants that belonged to my older sister Grace. And they had hearts all over them!

I'm on spring vacation, so I don't have much to remember. But because I don't have anything else to do right now except listen to The Destructor squawking about his bath, I find a sticky note and write a list of my own.

## ★ MY TO-DO LIST ★

1. Break a world record with Lonnie and Viva before the end of vacation.
2. Invent a way to keep The Destructor far away from me.
3. Feed the pigeons.

## THE PIGEONS

The Destructor is still fast asleep when I wake up the next morning. And it's not because he's worn out from the bath he had last night. It's because I wake up really early every morning to feed my neighbor's pigeons. Technically it's the first day of spring vacation, but that doesn't matter, because I still have a job to do. These pigeons almost helped me break a record. They're the same ones The Destructor borrowed the poo and feathers from and the same ones that live next door with Grumpy Pigeon Man.

As his nickname suggests, Grumpy Pigeon Man is a grumpy man. But last October for some reason he hired me to take care of his pigeons. I still don't know why he picked me out of my whole family, but I suspect it's because he knows I can put up with a lot. To be perfectly honest, I don't care why he picked me, because I just love those birds!

So now every morning I wake up at five thirty a.m. to feed them. My job is to pour water into the birds' drinking bowl and into their bath and give them their food. It's fun to watch them. The pigeons never fight. They share their food. They perch next to each other and coo. They flutter around but don't collide. And still each pigeon has its own personality. After all the time I've spent with them, I can really tell them apart.

They're like a family. A really, really *huge* family.

It's always amazing to me that they can live together so peacefully but that my family cannot. I mean, there are fifty-seven of them and only nine of us!

## LONNIE

When I get back from feeding the pigeons, Lonnie is waiting for me. Even for a best friend like Lonnie, this is early. And I can't imagine his parents agreed to drop him off.

Lonnie and I have been friends since kindergarten, when he taught me that drawing Star Wars stuff was as fun as playing Star Wars. Lonnie is training to be a Jedi Knight. Not a real one; he knows they don't actually exist. He just wants to be as much like one as he can. I think he's very successful, but in his own way, not like a repeat from the movies.

One of Lonnie's Jedi skills is that he can read my mind. So right away he says, "Jerome dropped me off." Jerome is his big brother, who is now dating my oldest sister, Sharon. Thinking about it makes me feel a little sick to my stomach, so instead I think of something else. The only other thing that comes to mind is the record for the largest bowl of porridge in the world. It's 3,042 pounds 6 ounces and is about as big as a hippopotamus. People are very dedicated about breaking world records. Otherwise, who would even dream of making so much porridge?!

After thinking about the porridge, my brain

goes back to Lonnie and Jerome, and I can't help wondering why Jerome dropped Lonnie off so early. Jerome is not known for his generosity. He is Lonnie's older brother, after all. Again, Lonnie reads my mind. "It was pretty simple," he says. "I told him he either brings me here now or I'd tell Sharon how he used to stick kidney beans up his nose, chase me around the house, and shoot them at me."

"*Snot beans!*" I say. "I remember that."

Lonnie nods.

"That was the funniest thing ever."

"It was," Lonnie says. "But it turns out that when you're seventeen it's not funny anymore. And even Jar Jar Binks would drive me here instead of having that story revealed to his *true love*."

"Ick," I say.

Lonnie shrugs. "I'm just glad I found his weakness."

I'm always impressed by Lonnie. He finds a peaceful way to work out everything.


## VIVA

Seconds later Viva shows up. Viva's life is very different from mine. She's an only child, which means she gets both privacy and attention. She says it's not so terrific, but she's never had to eat a mayonnaise sandwich for lunch because someone in her family stole the bologna and lettuce.

Anyway, Viva is pretty great and has some Jedi skills of her own, which could explain how we ended up friends. It definitely helps that she knows as much about Star Wars and *The Guinness Book of World Records* as we do.

She must be able to tell that I'm shocked that she's here as early as Lonnie because she says, "My parents were still in their pajamas. I mean, it might have been hours until they were ready, so I told them I'd bike."

"Were they okay about that?" I ask. Viva's parents are very strict with her.

She laughs. "Are you kidding? The chances of my parents letting me bike over here are about as likely as them letting me break the record for snapping the most mouse traps on my tongue in one minute. And Teddy, don't say what the record is because it's forty-seven."

Viva knows me pretty well.

Lonnie shakes his head. "No parent would want their kid to break that record."

Viva smiles. "Which is exactly why they drove me."

Sometimes Viva is so good at getting her way it's scary.

## JEDI MINDS CAN DO ANYTHING

"We should find something that's already a record and do it faster," Lonnie says.

Viva agrees. "We don't have time to make up a new record."

"Sounds good to me," I say as I pull out the two copies of *The Guinness Book of World Records* that I own. Picking a record to break is almost harder than breaking a record. Lonnie and Viva were really happy when I broke my world record, and after that we all wanted to break one together. So we came up with the plan to spend all of vacation doing exactly that. That way we could all have a record. Technically I'd have two, but that's okay.

We have only one week, which is not much time, especially because breaking a record is not easy, but I'm confident that together we can do it.

After all, Lonnie and Viva are awesome and can do anything when they put their Jedi minds to it.

## RECORD ATTEMPT

It took us a little longer than I thought it would, but we finally decided to beat the record for breaking the most eggs with our toes in thirty seconds.

The record is for 55 eggs. This means we'll each need 56 eggs, which adds up to a grand total of 165 eggs in all. Luckily, Mom buys every household item in bulk, so we always have about a million of everything. We even have an extra refrigerator and freezer in the basement.

I'll have to remember to write "buy more eggs"

on Mom's to-do list because after we're done, we'll only have three eggs left. But it will be *so* worth it!

## FAILED RECORD ATTEMPT

It turns out that breaking eggs with our toes is harder than we thought. We didn't get past five eggs.

After all that crushing, our toes couldn't bend, so we had to walk on our knees for hours, which might have been a better record to break, but now it's too late.

And even though we crushed the eggs over a bowl, Mom got mad. I guess she had a point. Who would want to eat eggs crushed by our toes

with the shells mixed in? Not even Dad, and he eats practically anything. I tell Mom that the good news is she doesn't have to add eggs to the grocery list.

Mom breathes deeply and then says, "I have other things to do over vacation than clean up after you three. So from now on you can attempt only one record a day."

I open my mouth to complain and Mom says, "One record a day or none at all."

I've lived with Mom long enough to know when she's serious. This is one of those times.

## PIGEON BOY

"Tomorrow," Viva says, "we've got to try something really good."

Lonnie says, "In the words of Yoda: 'Try not. Do, or do not. There is no try.'"

Viva punches him in the arm. "We still can only *do* one a day, so it better be good."

We decide to go to the aviary and pick tomorrow's record. Lonnie and Viva are the only other people who Grumpy Pigeon Man lets into his aviary. He's very picky about stuff like that.

I open the door and walk in. The Destructor

is here crouched down and covered in pigeon poo and feathers.

Again.

"Hi, Lonnie. Hi, Viva. Hi, Teddy," he says, and then goes back to covering every inch of his body.

And sure, it's terrible that he's slathered in poo and feathers, but right now the really *terrible* thing is that HE IS IN THE AVIARY AT ALL!

This is my place. My own private place. My no-one-else-in-my-family place. But most importantly, it's my Destructor-free place!

I'm about to tell him this, but Lonnie places a hand on my shoulder and says, "Don't go to the dark side."

And Viva adds, "He's only five."

"That's what everyone says," I say. "And they've been saying it since he was born."

Viva leans down to The Destructor, who's scraping up poo with a feather and gluing it to himself. "I thought you liked hanging out in the litter box."

The Destructor looks at her. "We call it a cat box."

"Whatever you call it, it's where you usually are."

Viva's right, of course: until a few days ago The Destructor's favorite place to hang out was in Smarty Pants's toilet. This was just plain gross, even in my family. Mom bought The Destructor his own cat box so Smarty Pants didn't have to share and The Destructor didn't get covered in cat poo. Mom was very pleased with herself about this.

"I've changed," The Destructor says as he stands up. "Pigeon Boy! Call me Pigeon Boy!" He starts flapping around, which is bad because the aviary is not very big. Lonnie and Viva duck out of the way, but I don't, and The Destructor runs straight into me, knocking me over and covering me in poo and feathers.

Again.

Viva looks at Lonnie and says, "Any words of wisdom, Yoda?"

Lonnie shakes his head. Just like me, he's speechless.

When we walk into the kitchen Mom says, "Why is your dad never home when stuff like this happens?"

"Mom," I say, "it's The Destructor you should worry about. He snuck into the aviary. Grumpy Pigeon Man—"

"Mr. Marney," she corrects me.

"Mr. Marney will be really mad."

"You're right," she says. "I'll have to talk to him about this."

I'm impressed with Mom; for once we're actually in agreement about The Destructor. But no matter what she says, I still have to keep an eye on him.

I don't care what he calls himself; he'll always be The Destructor to me.

## ★ MY TO-DO LIST #2 ★

1. Break a world record with Lonnie and Viva before the end of vacation.
2. Invent a way to keep The Destructor far away from me.
3. Feed the pigeons.
4. Invent a way to keep The Destructor out of the aviary.

## RECORD ATTEMPT #2

Because The Destructor distracted us yesterday, we sit around for a while trying to figure out a record.

Lonnie suggests jumping jacks and points to Bill Kathan's record for most jumping jacks in an hour (5,671).

"I've tried those jumping jacks before," I say. "They're harder than they look."

"Last time you weren't doing it with us," Viva says. "Remember, we're here to win."

"Anyway," Lonnie says, "Bill Kathan is old and we're ten years old. How can we lose?"

I can't help agreeing with Lonnie. We *definitely* have the age advantage in this record.

## FAILED RECORD ATTEMPT #2

It turns out I was wrong about having any advantage, but I was right about jumping jacks being

harder than you'd think, which is why we're lying on the ground in my backyard unable to move. Strange but true, I'm feeling a lot like the world's largest serving of cooked snails (2,449 pounds). Dead and mushy.

## KIDS THESE DAYS

When I go out to the aviary that afternoon, there is still no sign of The Destructor, which is great. Maybe he'll really be gone for good and I can cross that off my to-do list. Grumpy Pigeon Man comes out. He glares at me and then says, "You and your friends are trying to break more records, Tent Boy?"

"Yes, sir," I say. I hate being called Tent Boy, but there's no point in correcting him.

"Kids these days." He sighs. "You always want more. When I was your age, I was happy to have one of anything. One balloon. One scoop of ice cream. I only had one roller skate."

"What happened to the other one?" I ask.

"My sister had it, of course."

He walks back into his house before I can say anything. Considering the guy owns fifty-seven pigeons, I think it's a little weird that he complains about me wanting two world records.

Then again, he is Grumpy Pigeon Man. What do I expect?

## RECORD ATTEMPT #3

A good night's sleep really helps the muscles when you're trying to break a record. Unfortunately, it doesn't help us to think of what our next record should be. It's day three of spring vacation. We're in the aviary and we're stuck for ideas.

Finally, Viva says, "I've got it!"

I've learned from experience to be careful when Viva has an idea. Her ideas have gotten us into trouble before.

Viva says, "We make up our own record to break."

Lonnie says, "I thought we decided *not* to do that."

"Making up one is hard," I say.

"Oh brother!" Viva says. "If you're too afraid to try my idea then maybe I should do it alone." And then she stares straight at Lonnie and me and doesn't blink, and even though I know she's doing the Jedi mind trick, it totally works.

## FAILED RECORD ATTEMPT #3

Balancing the most books on our heads was not as good of an idea as Viva thought. First off, the most books we could balance was seven, and seven books will never get us into *The Guinness Book of World Records*.

The first time we tried, the books fell and almost crushed Smarty Pants. The second time the books crushed each of us. The third time the books crushed a lamp, and Mom told us that from now on all record breaking had to be done outside.

To be perfectly honest, we were

too bruised up to even walk outside, so we lay on the couch for the rest of the day and watched the first three Star Wars movies.

Star Wars makes everything better.

## RECORD ATTEMPT #4

Unbelievably, Lonnie and Viva show up early again the next day.

"If only you guys getting here could be a world record," I say as I pour everyone a bowl of cereal.

Lonnie pulls out two bags of marshmallows from his backpack. "How about this instead," he says.

"I love marshmallows," Viva says. "I could eat a million."

"The record is for eating twenty-five marshmallows in one minute," Lonnie says. "So we each need to eat twenty-six marshmallows in one minute."

"Is that all?" Viva says.

"We were born to break this record," I say.

And then we do a three-way high five, which actually fails horribly and we end up slapping each other's faces instead.

We'll need to work on that.

## FAILED RECORD ATTEMPT #4

Eating twenty-six marshmallows sounds easy, but after seven marshmallows my teeth stick together so much I think a tooth might get yanked out if I eat another. Of course I do eat another and another, because I'm trying to break a world record and Lonnie and Viva are still eating them.

It turns out that after nine marshmallows, chewing and breathing at the same time is pretty hard and swallowing is impossible. That's when I call it quits.

Lonnie stops at ten.

Viva eats eleven marshmallows and then throws up.

Mom was really, really happy we were outside.

Viva's mom wasn't happy about anything.

## ASHRITA FURMAN

The next morning Viva's mom calls. She says between the bruises and the vomit, it's been enough record breaking for one vacation, and she's sending Viva to her grandparents' house for the rest of the week!

This is wrong for so many reasons. I mean, Ashrita Furman has broken more than five hundred records and holds the record for most records held by one person at the same time. Does Viva's mom think that's too many records?

When I bring this up to Mom, she says, "Just because I let you act like a wild child doesn't mean every parent should do it."

And then Mom tells me that Viva's mom called Lonnie's mom, and now Lonnie is going to his grandparents', too!

This stinks! It totally ruins our chances of breaking a record before school starts again. And besides that, now what am I going to do for the rest of vacation?

This is bad. Very bad.

### ★ MY TO-DO LIST #3 ★

1. ~~Break a world record with Lonnie and Viva before the end of vacation.~~

2. Invent a way to keep The Destructor far away from me.
3. Feed the pigeons.
4. Invent a way to keep The Destructor out of the aviary.
5. Find something to do before I explode from boredom.
6. Break a world record with Lonnie and Viva.

## FIVE SISTERS IS MORE SISTERS THAN ANY KID SHOULD HAVE

In *The Guinness Book of World Records* there's a guy who holds the record for having the most cups kicked off his head in one minute (133 cups). Most of the time, living with five older sisters feels a lot like that. It's nerve-racking and startling, and really, you're always waiting for the time that the kicker messes up and kicks you in the head.

Eventually, it's bound to happen.

## MORE ABOUT MY SISTERS

1. **Sharon, the singer** (eighteen): All she ever wants to do is sing. Except now that she's dating Jerome, all she

wants to do is sing with him. Her favorite place to sing in our house is the upstairs bathroom.

**2. and 3. Caitlin and Casey, the twins** (fifteen): They used to be famous for pretending to be each other; now they are famous for their new business: Trash Trikes. They collect trash on wagons attached to their bikes. This might seem impressive, but what's really impressive is how bad they smell when they come home.

**4. Maggie, the runner** (fourteen): Maggie likes to run as much as Sharon likes to sing, but she smells a whole lot worse.

**5. Grace, the lemon** (thirteen): Grace's greatest joy in life is causing me pain. She did take the photographs that proved to the Guinness people I slept in a tent for 162 days. But the only reason she did that was to show the world what a nut-o her little brother is. (Her words, not mine.) She has no body odor issues.

## VENEZUELAN SKUNK FROG

The first day without Lonnie and Viva is both bad and good. It's bad because there is no record breaking. It's good because without record breaking, Grumpy Pigeon Man doesn't grump at me for wanting to break another record.

I also have to admit, it's not as boring as I thought it was going to be. I'm hanging out in the living room comparing the two copies of *The Guinness Book of World Records* that I own from different years. The Destructor drew all over one of them, but I can read through most of his scrawls.

It's really cool to compare them because a lot changes in these books from year to year. For example, only one book lists the most peaceful country (Iceland), the most rabbits pulled out of a hat in thirty minutes (300), or the most cucumbers cut from the mouth with a sword in one minute (27). One book lists all of the Rubik's Cube records, like the fastest time to solve it using only the feet (27.17 seconds) and most solved while riding a unicycle (28). I'm reading these and trying really hard to keep my mind off Sharon, who's in the upstairs bathroom singing, "The sun'll come out tomorrow! Bet your bottom dollar that tomorrow there'll be sun!"

She's there because a bunch of months ago she decided the bathroom had the best acoustics in the house, whatever acoustics are, and Mom and Dad allowed her to take it over whenever she wanted and for however long she wanted. This seems like a particularly bad parenting choice—even for my parents—because now we're only left with the downstairs bathroom, and it is the worst. The door sticks, and the toilet has been known to break and overflow (number six on my Destructor list). Also the upstairs bathroom is the only one with a bath and shower, which is important when you have smelly sisters like I do.

Anyway, I'm just reading about the fastest time to solve the most Rubik's Cubes in twenty-four hours (5,800) when Caitlin and Casey come home from their trash pickup. I grab my nose and try not to breathe, because they smell a lot like the Venezuelan skunk frog, the smelliest frog in the world. I guess it smells exactly like a skunk, even though it's a frog.

The smell lingers downstairs even after they've gone upstairs. They pound on the bathroom door, but Sharon just keeps singing. "When I'm stuck with a day that's gray and lo-onely!"

With a stink like this in the air, it's hard not to wish that tomorrow would come even sooner and that Sharon would stop singing and give up the bathroom.

## VENEZUELAN SKUNK FROG PART 2

Our house really gets lively when Maggie comes home from her run, smelling *worse* than the smelliest frog in the world. Who knew anything could smell worse than trash?

Maggie starts pounding too, but Sharon still doesn't stop singing about tomorrow.

Caitlin and Casey threaten to dump trash on Sharon's bed.

Maggie threatens to help, but it has no effect

on Sharon, who's now singing, "Tomorrow! Tomorrow! I love you, tomorrow! You're only a day away!"

And all I can do is tie those pillows around my head again, which protects my ears, but does nothing for my nose. I'm looking for a clothespin when Grace strolls in. She's carrying a new camera around her neck. It looks very professional, and I can't help wondering where she got it, because Mom and Dad wouldn't buy it for her.

"Did I tell you I'm working on the school newspaper?" she asks. "It's all thanks to the photos I took of you and your tent. They even gave me this camera!" I know Grace well enough to understand that even when she seems nice, she could attack at any moment.

"Great," I say, backing away from her. But before I can escape she stomps down on my foot and takes a picture of me hopping around holding my throbbing toes.

"I love action shots," she says.

"If you want action, go upstairs!" I say. "There's a lot of action up there!"

For once in her life Grace takes my advice.

## NOW YOU SEE HIM

I hop into the kitchen to tell Mom I'm going out to the aviary. Mom is reading the newspaper. She's either totally ignoring the racket coming from upstairs or totally oblivious. It's impossible to know which. But she finally looks up. "Oh," she says. I think for a second she might ask what's wrong with my foot, but she just looks around the room and says, "Have you seen Jake? He was here just a minute ago."

I realize another reason this was such a great day was that I had not seen The Destructor for any of it. "No, Mom. And if you haven't noticed, my foot is practically broken."

Of course she doesn't notice, because she's trying to find The Destructor. She starts with the cat box, his favorite spot, and then moves on to the kitchen cabinets, which were his favorite spots before the cat box. "Where could he be?" she asks mostly to herself.

That's when Caitlin, Casey, and Maggie all

come running downstairs complaining they need the bathroom, followed by Sharon complaining about interruptions, followed by Grace clicking away on her camera.

Sharon scowls at me and says, "It's your fault that Jerome had to go to his grandmothers'. We have an audition we were supposed to be practicing for."

"Audition?" Grace says. "I thought you were done with the school musical."

"It's a community theater production." The way Sharon says it you'd think it was Broadway. "You should write about it in your school paper."

Grace rolls her eyes. "I should get my earmuffs out."

Sometimes Grace is funny. "Wait a minute," Mom says. She sniffs the air deeply, then looks like she's going to upchuck. "Sharon, take a break from singing. These three need the bathroom more than you do right now."

"Mom!" Sharon starts to say.

"That's my decision. And whoever is not taking a bath needs to help me find Jake."

I slip out of the room while Mom's not looking. I've spent more time looking for The Destructor than any kid should have to. I go around to the aviary for a little peace and quiet and a lot less stink.

## THE BIGGEST MOUTH

Strange but true, the biggest mouth in the world is 6.69 inches wide, which happens to be bigger than my head! When I walk into the aviary, my mouth drops open just as big. Maybe bigger, but I don't have a ruler so I can't be sure.

Anyway, The Destructor is here all dressed up in poo and feathers. Again.

I thought Mom was going to take care of this.

Unfortunately, my mouth is open so big that when The Destructor flies past me—or should I say, pretends to fly past me—I get a mouthful of pigeon feathers. Yuck!

And the worst part is, I wasn't even trying to find him!

## SOMETHING HAS TO CHANGE

"Mom! I found him!" I call.

Mom rushes into the kitchen. "I knew you would. Where was he?" She stops talking, because as soon as she sees us she knows the answer.

"Mom," I say, "I thought you were going to stop this."

Dad walks in just then. "What's for dinner?" He stops because he also sees The Destructor. "I thought you were going to take care of this," he says to Mom.

Mom looks at Dad and says, "Sometimes you really say the wrong thing."

"What's going on?" Grace asks, bounding in from the living room. "Oh!" She starts clicking away. "I couldn't ask for better stuff. The school newspaper is going to love me!"

Dad says to Mom, "You'd better get him up to a bath."

Mom says, "Why am I always on bath duty?"

Dad's eyes get big and he says, "You know I would, but I've got to take the trash out." He leaves really quickly.

I might even say he runs. The Destructor tries to follow Dad, but Mom grabs him by a wing and stops him. "This way, Jake. Hey, no pecking!" she says as she leads him upstairs. "Something has to change."

"You can say that again," I say.

"Something has to change!" she yells.

I guess she really means it.

## IF I WERE TO LAND ON VENUS

*The Guinness Book of World Records* explains that if I were to land on Venus, I would instantly be:

1. Melted
2. Poisoned
3. Suffocated
4. Baked
5. Crushed
6. Dehydrated
7. Blown away

The rest of my vacation is worse than all of those things combined.

Mom decides that since I'm so bored without Lonnie and Viva, I am now in charge of keeping The Destructor out of the aviary.

I guess I should be happy that she's taking this seriously. But it would be nice if someone else played Go Fish with The Destructor besides me.

Strange but true, the record for being stuck in an elevator for the longest time is six days. I never thought that anything could feel so long, but it turns out that sitting in the kitchen playing thirty-three rounds of Go Fish feels longer.

Especially because The Destructor decided to

call it Go Pigeon, and he won every game except two, which probably explains why I finally threw all the cards on the floor and told him about a new game called 52 Pickup.

I never thought I'd say this, but I'm actually glad school starts tomorrow.

## EYEBROWS AND GUINEA PIGS

I am the first kid at school today and the first kid in our class line. I'm hoping Lonnie or Viva will be second and third, but they aren't. The only kid I see running across the blacktop is Lewis.

He comes to a shrieking stop behind me, dumps his bag down, and says, "How'd you get here first? I'm always in line first."

Lewis and I have been in the same class since first grade, but we never hang out.

We don't even talk that much, mostly because we always have other people to talk to. But right now there isn't anyone else except each other.

"You can go in front of me," I say.

"No thanks. The point is to be first."

I nod. I get what he means.

"So how was your vacation?" he asks, and then before waiting for an answer, he says, "Mine was good. I went to my grandparents'. They took me and my sister to a baseball game." He reaches into his backpack. "I caught the ball."

"Wow," I say. I've never been to a baseball game, and our family doesn't watch sports except whatever one Maggie is playing.

Lewis tosses the ball up and down. "How about you? You do anything?"

I shake my head. I could tell Lewis about breaking a world record, but I want to wait until Lonnie, Viva, and I break one together. Now, that'll be something great to share with our whole class.

As I'm thinking about this, a bunch of kids from our class show up.

Cornelio, Lewis's best friend, runs over. Then Ny and Serena. Ny moved here from Cambodia last year. She didn't speak much English at first, which is not surprising considering she grew up speaking a totally different language. But now she talks a lot. I can't imagine moving so far, leaving your friends and family, and then learning a whole new language! She's the bravest person I know.

Serena is Ny's best friend. She has the longest hair in our class. It doesn't come close to the record, which is 18 feet 5.54 inches, but when she tosses her hair over her shoulder, it's long enough to whack me in the face.

Right then Lonnie and Viva run up. They have to go in the back of the line because my class is *not*

okay with skipping ahead. I'm about to run back there with them when Ms. Raffeli walks outside and everyone hustles to get into a single line. Ms. Raffeli is a big fan of straight lines. She's also a big fan of not changing spots once we're in the line. But I think maybe she hasn't noticed me, because she's talking to the two other fourth-grade teachers, so I start to slip out of my place, but right then she says, "Teddy!"

I turn around. Her eyebrows jump up about as high as the guinea pig that broke the record for highest-jumping guinea pig. Patch only jumped 8.7 inches, which is not a lot unless you're either a guinea pig or eyebrows. Then it's really far.

I decide to stay where I am. Those eyebrows are very convincing.


## THE TEETH

Ms. Raffeli grabs my hand and says, "Come along, Teddy. There's so much to do."

As Ms. Raffeli pulls me down the hallway, I can't help thinking about Igor Zaripov, who broke the record for pulling the heaviest vehicle using only his teeth. The vehicle was a double-decker bus!

Right now I feel just like the bus, which can only mean one thing: Ms. Raffeli is the teeth.

## DISTRACTIONS

The second we walk into class, Ms. Raffeli claps her hands three times to get our attention. We freeze on the spot and look at her. "Hang up your backpacks and head straight to the rug."

Hanging up our backpacks is not as easy as you'd think. And to prove my point I get a backpack slammed in my face and an elbow in my ribs. I trip backward and land right on my butt.

Lonnie leans over and gives me a hand up. "You all right?" he asks.

"Yeah," I say.

Ms. Raffeli says, "I'm waiting."

Viva joins us. "As much as I love this school, hanging up my backpack is more annoying than meeting a Storm Trooper on the Death Star."

Ms. Raffeli says, "I'm still waiting."

Viva gets her backpack hung, then turns around to be sure Ms. Raffeli isn't looking at us. She whispers, "What's wrong with her today?"

"No idea," I say. "But she definitely has something on her mind."

"Teddy!" Ms. Raffeli shouts across the room. Her eyebrows are way up high again. "Don't get distracted."

I have to say, I find Ms. Raffeli's eyebrows very distracting. I feel the same way about my dad's ear hair, which is both gross and kind of amazing. I thought his ear hair was long until I compared it to the world record (7.1 inches). Dad's doesn't even come close. He actually lost by 6 inches!

Anyway, like I said, ear hair and Ms. Raffeli's eyebrows are very distracting.

## THE MOST IMPORTANT PROJECT

Lonnie, Viva, and I finally make our way to the rug. Everyone in our class is already seated, everyone except Angus, the hopper. He's crouched down by the backpacks with his shirt pulled over his knees, and he's hopping back and forth. Angus has a lot of energy. Ms. Raffeli usually lets him hop. She says, "If it helps Angus pay attention, he could hop to the moon and back and I wouldn't mind." But she doesn't let just anyone hop. Ms. Raffeli knows who needs to hop and who doesn't.

I wonder if Lonnie and Viva and I could break a record for hopping. Then I remember the jumping jacks. There's no way hopping will be any easier.

By the time I'm about to sit down, there aren't any spaces left next to either Lonnie or Viva, so I sit between Lewis and Serena.

Ms. Raffeli clears her throat. "Today we start the most important project of the year."

Cornelio says, "I thought the bird project was the most important."

"That's what I was going to say," Lewis says. Lewis always says this.

"I thought it was homes and habitats?" Serena says; then she flips her hair and whacks me in the face.

Ny says, "Remember the folktales unit we did at the beginning of the year?"

Jasmine B. says, "I like recess."

Jasmine H. says, "Recess isn't a project."

Jasmine B. says, "I know. I just like recess."

Angus hops over to the rug and says, "I like recess, too."

Ms. Raffeli quiets us all down. "We're not talking about recess."

Lewis leans over and says, "I totally know what we're doing."

The record for most swords swallowed at one time is 24. The chance of me breaking the record is as likely as Lewis knowing what we're about to study.

There is no way. Absolutely no way.

## MYSTERY BAG

Ms. Raffeli reaches behind her chair and pulls out a big black trash bag. When I say big, I mean the biggest.

"Mystery bag!" we all shout when we see it.

Ms. Raffeli is a serious teacher, but before we start a new unit, we always play mystery bag. "As usual," she says, "I've filled this bag with objects that are clues to our next project. You will each pull one out and try to guess what the project is.

Who wants to go first?"

All hands shoot up. All except Lewis, who says, "I don't want to ruin it for everyone else."

Max pulls out a plastic bag. "Are we studying shopping?"

Ms. Raffeli shakes her head.

"I totally know what it is," Lewis says.

Bekka takes out a rolled-up newspaper. It's the section with all the advertisements on it. "Shopping?" she asks.

Ms. Raffeli shakes her head.

Serena grabs a silver sparkly high-heel shoe.

The whole class goes real quiet. I'm sure we're all wondering the same thing: Does Ms. Raffeli actually own a pair of sparkly shoes? It's hard to picture that. Finally, Serena flips her hair and says, "Is it shopping?"

For the third time, Ms. Raffeli shakes her head.

When Angus pulls out a water bottle, he says, "You're sure it's not shopping? Because my mom just bought me a new water bottle while she was shopping yesterday. She says because I hop so much it's important to stay hydrated."

Ms. Raffeli says, "It's not shopping."

Angus hops over to his desk and takes a long sip out of his *new* water bottle.

Lewis leans over to me and says, "I really know what it is."

Ny pulls out a jar of grape jelly. Cornelio pulls out a soda can. And Viva finds a pair of pants. All three of them think it's shopping.

Ms. Raffeli has her head in her hands. "This was not my best mystery bag," she says.

I agree. Usually, we're much better at this game.

## I CAN'T BELIEVE IT

I pull out a bell. Jasmine B. finds a camera, and Jasmine H. a bag of popcorn. I ask if it's things we can make music with. Jasmine B. asks if it's things we can make art with. And Jasmine H. asks if Ms. Raffeli is sure it's not things to make art with because she's made a lot of art with popcorn. Ms. Raffeli shakes her head each time.

Lewis is not helping by telling me over and over again that he knows what the unit is about.

Lonnie reaches in and takes out a calculator. "Things that have nothing to do with each other?"

We all laugh except Ms. Raffeli, who looks around at our class. "There must be somebody who hasn't gone yet."

A few other kids raise their hand. Lewis says, "I can't believe you guys haven't guessed it yet."

Ms. Raffeli was about to pick Chrystal but instead points to Lewis.

"Me?" he says. "Sure." He walks to the bag and reaches really far down. You can tell he touches something icky because his face scrunches up; then he pulls out an old banana. "Yuck!" he says, and drops it back into the bag. "Well?" Ms. Raffeli says. "Any ideas?"

"Inventions." Lewis says this like it's the most

obvious thing in the world.

"Inventions?" I say. "How is *that* a bag of inventions?"

"Finally!" Ms. Raffeli beams. "Our next and most important project is the inventors' fair."

I can't believe it. Lewis did know!

"Of course," Lonnie says, hitting his head with his hand. "The inventors' fair. How could I forget?"

"Hey, Lewis! How is a banana an invention?" Jasmine B. asks.

"Seriously," Jasmine H. says, "how *is* a banana an invention?"

Viva says, "Forget the banana, how did he know it was inventions at all?"

"Because the fourth grade does an inventors' fair every year!" Lonnie explains.

I guess I was wrong about Lewis not knowing the project, but I don't care, because I'm still never going to swallow 24 swords.

That would just hurt too much.

## A SIDE I'VE NEVER SEEN BEFORE

Ms. Raffeli tucks the bag of *inventions* behind her desk and settles us back down.

Viva raises her hand and starts talking. "Ms. Raffeli, I love inventors' fairs. Last year we did one at my old school. The theme was camping, so we all had to make inventions that could be used on a camping trip." Ms. Raffeli's eyebrows are practically touching the top of her head, but Viva doesn't notice and keeps going. "I made a battery-powered sneaker dryer. The Maxley twins invented a flashlight marshmallow cooker. You could use it as a flashlight or to cook marshmallows. It was a very competitive year. At least that's what my mom said."

"A flashlight marshmallow cooker?" Lonnie says. "That's the best invention I've ever heard of."

"It's not as good as it sounds," Viva says.

I look over at Ms. Raffeli, who doesn't look so happy with this conversation, but at least her eyebrows have gone down, which gives me the courage to ask Viva a question. "Who won?"

Viva smiles. "I did, of course!"

"Really?" Lonnie says. "You won for a sneaker dryer over a marshmallow flashlight cooker?"

Viva looks at him as if he's crazy. "Do you know how stinky wet sneakers are? Also on the day of the fair the flashlight marshmallow cooker didn't work, but my battery-powered sneaker dryer did." She closes her eyes and smiles. "I love winning," she says.

This is a side to Viva I've never seen. I've seen her be pushy, like when she started sitting with Lonnie and me at lunch and wouldn't go away no matter how much I tried to make her. I've seen her be brave, like the time she got us to sneak into Grumpy Pigeon Man's avi-ary without asking permission first. But there's something different about this winning thing.

Ms. Raffeli says, "Viva, I'm glad to hear you say that. And this year that is exactly what we will do. Win."

I have to admit, this is also a side of Ms. Raffeli I've never seen, but the look in her eye totally reminds me of Grace right before she attacks my feet.

It's definitely scary.

## INVENTIONS VS. WORLD RECORDS

Jasmine B. says, "I still want to know how a banana is an invention."

Jasmine H. nods her head. "Me too."

Ms. Raffeli says, "Wild bananas are nothing like the bananas we eat now. They used to be small and full of seeds. They've been transformed by food inventors."

"Is that a real job?" Jasmine B. asks.

"Yes," Ms. Raffeli says. "They are scientists who focus on food. Finding ways to make the things we eat more delicious or nutritious."

Jasmine H. says, "I want that job."

Ms. Raffeli claps her hands. "Now, back to our inventors' fair."

But Jasmine B. interrupts again. "What about the pants? How are they an invention?"

Ms. Raffeli's eyebrows pop up. It's easy to tell she'd like to be talking about something else, but she is the one who put the mystery bag together, so she has only herself to blame for all of our questions. She takes a deep breath, leans back in her chair, and says, "Who can answer that?"

Viva raises her hand. "People didn't always wear pants. Someone had to invent this thing that we put both our legs into and call *pants*."

Ms. Raffeli nods.

Lonnie says, "The sewing machine we use to sew them together is an invention."

Ms. Raffeli nods again.

"Then there's the zipper," Ny says. "That's an awesome invention."

Serena says, "And the dye used to color the pants is invented."

Cornelio raises his hand. "The cotton the jeans are made from is an invention, too."

Lewis says, "I was going to say that."

I raise my hand. "I have to admit, I've never thought about a pair of pants like that before, but a lot of small inventions go into one big invention. It's a lot like breaking a world record. No one just starts out being able to juggle three bowling balls. First you have to know how to juggle, then you have to be strong, then you add the bowling balls. *Then* you break the record for most bowling balls juggled! Thinking it through like this, you realize how hard juggling bowling balls actually is." I stop talking and look at Ms. Raffeli, who says, "Could we get through one lesson without it turning into a world record?"

She has a point. I do get distracted by world records. A lot.

## ★ MY TO-DO LIST #4 ★

1. ~~Break a world record with Lonnie and Viva before the end of vacation.~~
2. Invent a way to keep The Destructor far away from me.
3. Feed the pigeons.
4. Invent a way to keep The Destructor out of the aviary.
5. ~~Find something to do before I explode from boredom.~~
6. Break a world record with Lonnie and Viva.
7. Think up a world record to break with Lonnie and Viva.


## WHO WAS DISTRACTING WHO?

Ms. Raffeli stands up and shows us the calendar. "Over the next month, we shall be making our inventions." She puts a big red $X$ on the date of the inventors' fair. "In four weeks we will compete against the other fourth-grade classrooms and present our inventions."

Ms. Raffeli explains how she will put us into small groups and that each group will create one invention. You can see everyone get antsy about this, because everyone wants to work with a friend. I'm not worried at all. Lonnie, Viva, and I have worked really well together the whole year. There's no way Ms. Raffeli would separate us. We're an amazing team.

Viva interrupts. "What's the theme?"

Ms. Raffeli shakes her head. "We don't have one."

"That's weird," Viva says.

"Not really," Ms. Raffeli says. "You can invent whatever interests you. The only rule is that all of the inventions have to be made entirely out of recycled materials. So, cardboard boxes, fabric, wire, wood, nails, cans, bubble wrap. Anything at all that you find sitting around your house can be used, but you can't buy anything new for the project."

Lewis says, "I knew that." I look at him like, *how is that possible?* He says, "What? I did."

Ms. Raffeli's eyebrows go up and she says, "Teddy, no distractions."

And I can't help wondering, who was distracting who?


## WEIRDEST FAIR EVER

Viva raises her hand. "Who decides who the winner is?"

"The students in the school will vote for the winning invention."

"What's the prize for winning?" Angus asks.

"The prize is the joy of winning," Ms. Raffeli says.

Viva says, "But really, there's got to be a prize."

"Sometimes," Ms. Raffeli says, "the process is enough."

"So there's no actual prize?" Viva asks. "No gift certificate? No pizza party?"

Jasmine B. says, "I like prizes."

Jasmine H. says, "Me too."

"That's what I was going to say." Lewis shrugs.

Ms. Raffeli shakes her head. "There is no prize."

Viva smiles. "How about a pajama party?"

"We don't need a prize to win."

"Ice cream party?" Viva asks.

"Viva, there is no prize, has never been a prize, and never will be a prize."

Lonnie asks, "Have you won the inventors' fair a lot?"

Ms. Raffeli's eyebrows pop

up. "I have never won the inventors' fair. But this year will be different. I'm sure."

"I bet a prize would help," Viva says.

Ms. Raffeli clears her throat. "It's time for snack." Which is her way of saying this conversation is over.

We all stand up to get our snacks, and then under her breath Viva adds, "This is the weirdest inventors' fair ever."

## VIVA, HER MOM, AND MY STALE SANDWICH BREAD

After snack, Ms. Raffeli talked more about the inventors' fair, we did some math and reading, and finally it was time for lunch, which is my favorite part of the school day because Lonnie, Viva, and I can talk without anyone interrupting us. We always sit in the cafeteria at the table closest to the trash cans. Trust me, nobody else wants to sit here.

Strange but true, the record for most people to squeeze into a Mini (one of the smallest cars in the world) is 27. Living with my family is like being stuck in that car all the time. There's no escaping them, there's no peace and quiet, and you usually have a foot pressed against your nose.

If your life was like that, then all you would want is to have twenty minutes alone at lunch with your best friends.

"Are we breaking a record today?" I ask.

Lonnie smiles. "I already told my mom I was going to your house after school."

"Me too," Viva says.

"Really?" I ask.

"She said I'm allowed to go but I'm not allowed to get hurt. Or sick. My mom definitely doesn't want me doing anything that will make me sick."

We all take out our sandwiches. Lonnie says, "Looks like there was some bologna left today."

"That's a plus," I say, biting into it. I have to chew twice as much as Lonnie or Viva because the bread is so stale. According to *The Guinness Book of World Records* the first rocks on Earth were formed 4 billion years ago. Clearly my sandwich bread was formed at the same time. I even have to take a gulp of milk before I can speak again. "Okay," I say. "So what record won't hurt you or make you sick?"

Lonnie says, "Does a record like that even exist?"

"Probably not," Viva says. "So we should just do what we want. I'll take care of my mom."

I wish she could do the same for my sandwich bread.


## FRISBEES

It was a long first day back. We talked a lot about the inventors' fair. It's finally the end of the day, and we're packing up our stuff. I'm feeling extra restless because Lonnie, Viva, and I haven't come up with a record to break. If we can't think of anything, it will just be a waste of an afternoon.

It turns out I can't think of a single record that won't hurt us or make us sick. While I'm stuffing my lunchbox into my backpack, a notebook swishes past my head.

"See, Cornelio," Lewis says, "I told you notebooks fly really well."

And suddenly, thanks to Lewis and his flying notebook, I think of a record. "The most Frisbees caught behind the back in one minute. It's only twenty-four! We can beat that."

Viva smiles. "I am an excellent Frisbee thrower."

"Not as good as me," Lonnie says.

I'm not sure if I'm good or bad, because I've never actually played Frisbee. But how hard can it be? It's just a piece of plastic.

## FAILED RECORD ATTEMPT #5

What I've learned from this record is that throwing a piece of plastic is more complicated than I thought.

"Lonnie," Mom says, handing him a clean tissue, "keep the pressure on your nose and the bleeding will stop."

Mom passes Viva a bag of frozen peas. "We don't want you getting a black eye, Viva."

"It's so cold," Viva says.

Grace, who's been watching us the whole time and taking pictures for the school newspaper, says, "Of course it's cold. It's frozen." She clicks away.

"What about me?" I ask.

"What's wrong with you?" Mom asks.

"I sprained my wrist."

Mom wiggles my hand back and forth. "I'd be more worried about Viva's mother than about your wrist." And she walks away.

Sometimes I don't think Mom takes my problems seriously.

## THE KNOT IN MY THROAT

After Lonnie and Viva leave, I go out to the aviary to feed the birds. I need a little time with just the pigeons, but when I walk in I get something totally different.

The Destructor. Alone. Crouched on a bucket like a pigeon on a perch.

Before I can speak, he says, "Look!" And he stands up. He's wearing some kind of costume. There's a hood with a beak that hangs down over his face. There are fake gray feathers sewn onto the shirt. He spreads his arm and I see wings. There's even a giant *PB* drawn on the front. "It stands for Pigeon Boy," he says, as if I couldn't figure that out for myself. "Mom made it for me."

"Why are you here?"

"Mr. Marney said I can come over whenever I want. He said I can help you. He said I'm big enough now." He stands on a bucket smiling at me, as if I should be so happy that he's taking over my aviary, taking over my job.

Strange but true, the biggest skateboard in the world is 36 feet long by 8 feet 8 inches wide and 3 feet 7.5 inches tall.

The knot in my throat is bigger than that skateboard. And it hurts so much I can't even yell at him.

## SHOULD HAVE KNOWN

When I go to find Mom she's mowing the lawn. Mowing the lawn is not something Mom does. It's one of Dad's jobs.

I bring up my complaints about The Destructor and she says, "It's just a passing phase, Teddy. Ignore him."

A little while later, I catch Dad filling the washing machine with dirty clothes.

"Do you even know how to do that?" I ask.

"Ha, ha," he says. "Very funny."

I'm not actually joking, but I don't tell him that. Instead I tell him all about how The Destructor is taking over the aviary.

"He's just a little kid, Teddy. Don't let him bother you."

I should have known. When it's a problem I have, they don't care, but wait until it's about me cleaning my room—then they'll be bothered.

## DON'T SAY A WORD

That night at dinner The Destructor is still wearing his pigeon costume and eating under the table in what he calls a *nest*. I call it my favorite sweater, which is now too dirty and gross to ever wear again. I'm taking a bite of my food when I get shot with a wad of wet paper towel. The Destructor's holding a slingshot and smiling at me.

"Mom!" I say.

"He wants to keep the pigeons safe. I think it's sweet," Mom says as she passes him a plate of food.

"I think it's dangerous, but no one listens to me."

"What's with the outfit?" Caitlin and Casey ask together. No matter how many times they say the same thing at the same time, it's always weird.

Mom says, "Jake and I came to an agreement. I make him a pigeon costume and he stops making one for himself."

Grace takes out her camera and starts clicking.

"Not at the table," Dad says.

"But I need three stories to share with the newspaper tomorrow," Grace says. "I want to make the front page of the next issue, and if this isn't a good story, I don't know what is."

Maggie puts down her fork. "You should do a story about the track team."

Grace rolls her eyes. "Writing about people running around a track is not the kind of story I want to tell."

Caitlin and Casey say, "How about Trash Trikes?"

"Maybe," Grace says.

Just then Sharon walks in.

"How was the audition?" Mom asks.

"Great. By tomorrow I'll be the next Annie."

"Aren't you a little old to be Annie?" Grace asks. "Isn't she supposed to be ten?"

Sharon is too distracted by The Destructor to answer. This is the first time she's seen his new outfit.

"Don't say a word," Mom says.

And because Sharon is so happy about her audition, she doesn't say a word, not to The Destructor or to Grace. This is extremely unusual because Sharon has a lot to say about most things. But then The Destructor reaches up for the mashed potatoes and his wing knocks the bowl of gravy right into Sharon's lap.

It's amazing how much she has to say now that she's coated in gravy.

## ADMIRAL ACKBAR

Early the next morning, I go out to feed the birds.

This is my favorite time of day. No one else is awake. Grumpy Pigeon Man never comes out, and I know The Destructor isn't here. I left him in our room fast asleep.

I'm happy to be alone with the pigeons. I feed them and water them and then turn a bucket over to watch them. I sit very still so they'll land on me. This was not easy to learn, but now I'm a champion at sitting and not jiggling.

Lando Calrissian flies down and lands on my knee. I pet his head. Lonnie, Viva, and I named a bunch of the pigeons after Star Wars characters. C-3PO paces back and forth right at my feet, like he's got something to say but can't figure out how.

Grace thinks the pigeons are gross; I think they're cool.

Admiral Akbar flies down onto my other knee. Lando Calrissian walks up and down my leg. Admiral Ackbar copies him. Their heads bob up and down. And then all of a sudden Admiral Ackbar lunges at Lando Calrissian. His wings beat and he starts to peck. I stand up and Lando

Calrissian flies off, landing on a perch. Admiral Ackbar struts around on the ground before taking his place on a different perch.

C-3PO stays on the ground and coos. He doesn't sound anything like C-3PO, but his coos feel like something C-3PO would say.

I've never seen two pigeons fight before. It makes me sad. They're not supposed to fight. I'll have to remember to ask Grumpy Pigeon Man what's going on.

I stand up to leave just as the door swings open. It's The Destructor, in his pigeon costume.

"Why didn't you wake me?" he asks, as if there was some kind of plan. As if I want him here.

If I had wings and a beak, I'd scare him away like Admiral Ackbar did to Lando Calrissian. Instead, I shake my head and walk past him. Lonnie has been trying to teach me that sometimes when you're angry, it's much safer not to say a word. He says it's the Jedi way.

I'm sure he's right, but it certainly doesn't make me feel better.


## SWEATY AND STINKY

Ms. Raffeli has us go straight to our seats as soon as we walk into class. "Today," she says, "we become winners. We become inventors. We make history." This time her eyebrows float up just like the record for the highest flight of a hot air balloon (68,986 feet), and instead of being startling those eyebrows are inspiring.

Ms. Raffeli explains that she has taken out a pile of books on inventors and inventions and we should each pick one out, read it silently, and be ready to share our thoughts with the rest of the class.

I'm reading about Thomas Edison right now.

It's one of those old, boring books with black-and-white pictures and a lot of words, and it makes me feel a little restless. I'm only on page two when I get to a word I don't know. I lean over to Lonnie and Viva. "What's a patent?" I ask.

Lonnie says, "It's the thing that proves that a person invented what they say they invented."

"Why would anyone lie about inventing something?" I ask.

"Teddy, less talking, more reading," Ms. Raffeli says from across the room.

I nod and go back to my book. Thomas Edison always gets credit for the lightbulb, but it turns out people had been working on lightbulbs for fifty years. He did something to make it better, but to be perfectly honest, I don't understand *what*.

Edison also holds 2,332 patents for all his inventions, which must be some kind of world record, even though I've never found it in *The Guinness Book of World Records*.

As usual, thinking about world records gets me thinking about *breaking* a world record. But I stop myself because Ms. Raffeli walks by. I can tell that this whole inventors' fair is really important to her, so I go back to my reading.

In the next chapter there are a bunch of quotes by Thomas Edison. I have to admit, he said some cool things:

"Our greatest weakness lies in giving up.
The most certain way to succeed is
always to try just one more time."

"I have not failed, I've just found
ten thousand ways that won't work."

"Genius is one percent inspiration
and ninety-nine percent perspiration."

The last one is a little weird because perspiration is sweat, and sweat is stinky, and why would you want to be stinky unless you couldn't help it? And then for no reason at all I'm thinking about how breaking world records and inventing are really similar, because lots of times trying to break a record gets you sweaty and stinky. And that gets me thinking about what world record Lonnie, Viva, and I could break that is not stinky or sweaty.

And this time Ms. Raffeli is not around to distract me!

## POSSIBILITIES

That's when I remember the garlic record. It's for the most garlic eaten in a minute. This seems pretty cool because even though the record breaker ate 34 cloves and that sounds like a lot, it actually isn't, because each piece of garlic probably has twenty cloves, and each clove is tiny, so it's probably only two mouthfuls. I'm sure we could all force two mouthfuls down to break a record.

This is it. This is our record!

"Lonnie," I say. "Viva. I've got the perfect record."

Lonnie doesn't hear me. This is not surprising because he's reading about someone called Nikola Tesla, and when he starts reading something interesting, he really gets into it. He doesn't look up from his book but reads out loud. "It turns out Tesla and Edison were total rivals. Tesla created an electrical system, but Edison took the credit. Tesla also invented a laser, a way of taking x-rays, and the first remote-controlled boat."

Viva looks up. "I'm reading about women inventors," she says. "In 1903, Mary Anderson invented windshield wipers. And the first flat-bottomed paper bag was invented by Margaret Knight in 1868."

"I've never thought about a paper bag being an invention," Lonnie says.

"Me neither," Viva says.

"Put your books down," I say. "I've got a record for us to break."

"Teddy Mars!" Ms. Raffeli says. "How many times do I have to ask you not to distract your friends?"

"If I'm going to be honest, I guess quite a lot." I think Ms. Raffeli should appreciate my honesty about the situation.

Instead she says, "Switch seats with Max." Clearly proving she does not appreciate my honesty.

## THE SUN WILL COME OUT TOMORROW

It's so weird to sit at a new seat that all day long I have a hard time paying attention. The room looks different from here, and the voices sound different because they're not Lonnie's and Viva's. Even the desk feels different, because it's taller than mine. All these differences make my sharing what I learned about Thomas Edison not go well. Which means Ms. Raffeli has me eat lunch in the classroom so I can write up what I did learn. Unfortunately, this takes me longer than I thought it would, because it turns out I learned quite a lot about Thomas Edison. I ended up missing recess. Ms. Raffeli felt really badly about this, but by then there wasn't anything to do. And the worst part was that I still hadn't told Lonnie and Viva about the garlic idea.

I was still distracted after recess, so I missed the homework directions, and now while everyone else piles out of the classroom, I have to wait for Ms. Raffeli to tell me the homework again. But, of course, I'm distracted by everyone piling out of the classroom, so I don't hear what she says.

When I ask her to repeat herself, she says, "Just go home, Teddy. Tomorrow is bound to be better."

And by the time I get outside, I don't see Lonnie and Viva anywhere.

Ny and Serena run up to me. "Hey, Teddy!" Serena says. "Lonnie and Viva were waiting, but they didn't know how long you'd be, so they went to Lonnie's."

Ny says, "They said to call them when you get home."

Serena flips her hair right in my face and they run off.

So now I'm walking home alone and for some reason I've got that song that Sharon keeps singing—the one about the sun coming out tomorrow—stuck in my head. I sure hope Ms. Raffeli is right about tomorrow because today was downright gloomy.


## NO MESSAGE

As soon as I get home I call Lonnie. Jerome answers but won't give the phone to Lonnie. He says, "It's payback for the snot-bean threats." And he hangs up.

I decide to call Viva's just in case they are there, but her mom answers and says, "Sorry, Teddy, Viva's at Lonnie's. Want to leave a message?"

"No thanks," I say. Sometimes it's better not

to say anything. I have a feeling that if I told Viva's mom about my garlic idea, she would not like it and she'd actually put a stop to it. Can you imagine if Thomas Edison had a mom like Viva's? He probably wouldn't have invented a thing!

At this moment, I realize that I've got to find a place we can break a record, because after the Frisbee attempt, we're not allowed to do it at my house. We can't do it at Lonnie's. His parents both work and have a rule about having only one friend over in the afternoons. Obviously, Viva's house is *not* an option.

There's got to be a solution to this problem, and thanks to Thomas Edison's quote about inspiration and perspiration, I'm not giving up until I find it!

Unless I get too stinky. Then I might take a break for a shower.

### ★ MY TO-DO LIST #5 ★

I take out my to-do list number four. It's getting way too long and messy so I throw it away and start a new list.

1. Invent a way to keep The Destructor far from me.
2. Invent a way to keep The Destructor out of the aviary.
3. Get my old desk back.
4. Figure out *when* and *where* Lonnie and Viva and I can break the record.
5. Break a world record with Lonnie and Viva.

## ENOUGH ON YOUR PLATE

After I don't talk to either of my friends, I go out to feed the pigeons.

"Freeze, Tent Boy," Grumpy Pigeon Man says as I open the door. I'm used to the way Grumpy Pigeon Man bosses me around, so I freeze, but then I look up and see The Destructor in his pigeon costume kneeling in front of a bunch of pigeons nestled on the ground.

"Close the door, Tent Boy," Grumpy Pigeon Man says to me, then turns back to The Destructor. "It's that one," he says, pointing to Admiral Ackbar, the pigeon that was acting strange yesterday. "You want to scoop that one up."

The Destructor walks over and scoops it up

just like Grumpy Pigeon Man said. I nearly fall over when Grumpy Pigeon Man says, "Good."

Grumpy Pigeon Man giving a compliment is as rare as the record for the fastest time to make a bologna, cheese, and lettuce sandwich all with your feet (1 minute 57 seconds). Only one person has ever broken that record.

"Now bring him over here." Grumpy Pigeon Man takes Admiral Ackbar and wraps his arms around him. The bird's little feet stick out from between his hands. Grumpy Pigeon Man strokes Admiral Ackbar on the head and says to The Destructor, "I have to keep an eye on this guy. He's getting a little feisty."

I'm about to ask him why Admiral Ackbar is acting like this when The Destructor says, "I'll keep an eye on him."

"Good boy," Grumpy Pigeon Man says. "And if he starts attacking, you go in and shoo them apart."

I don't know why

Grumpy Pigeon Man is giving lessons to The Destructor and not to me.

"What about me?" I say.

Grumpy Pigeon Man looks over. "I think you've got enough on your plate. You can let your little brother take care of this."

"Yeah," The Destructor says, "I'll take care of this."

I can't believe it! The Destructor is driving me crazy.

I'm the kid who works for Grumpy Pigeon Man, not him. So why is it that I'm the one who feels like I'm in *their* way?

## IS THIS A TEST?

There's only one thing that takes my mind off The Destructor, and that's breaking a world record. I need to find garlic, and I've got to figure out where we can break the record. I decide to look for garlic first, because that's easier.

"Mom?" I ask when I walk into the kitchen. "Do we have any garlic?"

As usual, Mom is reading the newspaper, which means she doesn't hear me, so I ask again.

She points to a white pot that sits on the counter behind the sink. I open it and can't believe my luck. There's more than enough garlic for us to break the record. Grace walks in right then, and before I could say *Guinness Book of World Records* she slams her foot down on my foot, then she slams her foot down on my other foot, then she jumps up and slams both her feet down on both my feet. It's so painful that all I can do is collapse.

As usual, Mom does not look up from her newspaper.

"What was that for?" I gasp. Even for Grace that's a little overboard.

"The first one," she says, "is for being born. The second one is for breaking a world record."

"And the third one? The double toe breaker?" I manage to ask.

"That is for the editor of the school paper deciding my first story—my front-page story, my *big moment*—is going to be all about *you*! You and your dumb record!"

I can tell she'd like to stomp again, but as long as I'm curled up on the floor she can't get to my feet, so I stay where I am.

Just then Dad comes in. He's as oblivious as Mom when it comes to my suffering, so he doesn't say anything either. He walks up to Mom, gives her a peck on the cheek, and says, "What's for dinner? I'm starved."

Now Mom looks up from her paper. "I cleaned the gutters today," she says.

Dad says, "Thanks. Now I don't have to."

"It wasn't as hard as I thought," Mom says.

"I'm glad," Dad says. "So what's for dinner?"

Mom says, "I don't know. What's for dinner?"

Dad looks at Mom. "Is this a test?" he asks.

"Not at all, but I thought you could make dinner tonight since I cleaned the gutters."

Dad stares at Mom and Mom stares at Dad. They keep staring at each other.

Grace and I stare at Mom and Dad. There's definitely something going on between my parents, but I have no idea what that is. And then Grace says, "What's wrong with those two?"

"I don't know," I say. "But if they keep it up, we'll be the ones making dinner."

## OH!

"Dinner is served!" Dad says.

I sit down at the table because even if I'm not sure I want to eat what Dad's made, I know I have to.

Sharon storms in. She's scowling and dumps her bag on the floor.

"Sharon?" Mom says.

"I don't want to talk!" Sharon yells.

"What happened?" Mom says.

Sharon clenches her teeth and says, "Jerome got Daddy Warbucks."

"That's great!" Mom is smart enough to know if Sharon is this mad it can only mean one thing, but she still asks, "What about you?"

Sharon can barely get the words out. "I'm an orphan."

"Oh," Mom says.

## OH! PART 2

Caitlin and Casey come in, but they're scowling at each other. Caitlin pushes her way past Casey and sits at a chair. "I *do* pick up more trash than you," she says.

Casey says, "How can you say that?"

"Because," Caitlin says, "half of your bins are empty all the time."

"That is not true," Casey says. "The truth is you fill up your bins with all those plastic bags. They take up a lot of space, but they're as heavy as a fly."

"Oh yeah?" Caitlin says.

"Yeah!" Casey says.

Mom says, "What's going on? You two never fight."

"Well, we are now!" they say at the same time.

"Oh," Mom says.


## OH! PART 3

Maggie walks in. She's been at practice and does not look happy. I'm not happy because she really smells bad. "I can't believe it," she says, sitting down and yanking off her sneakers. "I lost the hundred meters to Bella Colon by a fourth of a second."

"Which school does she run for?" Mom asks.

"Ours. She's in my grade."

"So it's not so bad to lose, right?" Mom says. "She's on your team."

"Are you kidding?" Maggie says. "I don't care what school she goes to, I don't want to lose to anyone."

"Oh," Mom says.


## OH! PART 4

"Oh," Sharon says after her first bite.

"Oh," Caitlin and Casey say.

"Oh," Maggie says.

"Oh," Grace says.

"Oh," I say. I feel like I might throw up.

Dad says, "Can't someone say anything else?"

"I love it!" The Destructor says. "It tastes like birdseed." And he flaps his wings for emphasis.

Besides the fact that I'm pretty sure Dad was not trying to make birdseed, I can't help wondering how The Destructor knows what birdseed tastes like.

Mom looks at Dad and says, "You definitely need more practice."

"Hold it right there," I say. "You're going to let

him do this again?"

Dad says, "If your Mom can clean the gutters, then I can cook dinner."

"It's the only way he'll learn," Mom says.

"Why is it so important he learns to cook? You've been doing great so far."

Mom rolls her eyes and says to Dad, "And don't forget, tonight is Jake's bath."

"Great," Dad says. "I'll do the dishes."

"No, you will bathe him, and I will do the dishes."

"Oh," Dad says. There's clearly nothing else to say.

## ★ MY TO-DO LIST #6 ★

For some reason being with the pigeons always helps with my thinking. So this morning after I feed them I sit down on a bucket and pull out my to-do list. Even though I'm new to the whole to-do list thing, I know the goal is to cross items off, which, so far, has not gone as well as I thought it would.

Admiral Ackbar flies down and sits on my knee. My biggest problem is figuring out where to break the record. And then it hits me! It's perfect, and I'll even get to cross something off my list.

So now my list looks like this:

1. Invent a way to keep The Destructor far from me.
2. Invent a way to keep The Destructor out of the aviary.
3. Get my old desk back.
4. ~~Figure out *when* and *where* Lonnie and Viva and I can break the record.~~
5. Break a world record with Lonnie and Viva.
6. Break a world record with Lonnie and Viva DURING RECESS.


## SOMERSAULTS AND UNDERWEAR

Ms. Raffeli is the kind of teacher who is always calm and in control, and except for those eyebrows, she's not scary at all. I am really happy to say that Ms. Raffeli let me sit at my cluster with Lonnie and Viva!

(That's another thing I can cross off my list when Ms. Raffeli isn't looking. I don't want to do anything that will change her mind.)

I promised not to distract anyone, so I haven't talked to Lonnie and Viva about the garlic plan yet. It's hard to wait, especially since the garlic is right in my backpack, but I am not going to mess it up this time. And anyway, I have to remember to order school lunch. Getting school lunch is very strange for me and has only happened once before. That time, Mom was throwing up all over the house. Who wants a lunch made by an upchucker? That's just gross.

But I need school lunch because after all these years of Mom making my lunch, today she let Dad make it. After last night's dinner, the lunch he packed did not seem like a good idea. So I pretended to forget it.

Strange but true, there is a record for most somersaults into underpants in 90 seconds. They don't tell us how many somersaults he did, but they do tell us how many pairs of underpants he got into: 95.

I can honestly say I know how that guy felt, because trying to remember to order school lunch while also trying not to distract Lonnie and Viva is very similar to breaking that record. Not only do you have to keep track of everything you're supposed to do, but you have to do it while wearing 95 pairs of underpants at one time. I mean, really, that has got to be uncomfortable.

Anyway, because I'm thinking about somer-saulting and underwear, I totally forget to order the school lunch.


## SCHOOL LUNCH

Ms. Raffeli claps her hands. "In the words of Shakespeare, 'To be, or not to be, that is the ques-tion!' In the words of me: to win, or not to win, there is no question!"

"Ms. Raffeli," I say. "Did you get my name down for the school lunch?"

"This is no time to talk about lunches, Teddy." Her eyes have that faraway look that I get when I'm contemplating how to get rid of The Destructor. I know this look well. I know she didn't really hear my question, so I say, "I need lunch."

She says, "Teddy, no interruptions. Serena, take the attendance and lunch order to the office."

As Serena walks past me, I ask her to put my name down for a lunch. She grabs my pencil, leans over my desk, and writes my name. Then she flips her hair out of her face and right into mine. This one time I don't mind, because at least she heard me, which is more than I can say about my teacher.

Lonnie looks at me. "You hate school lunch."

"I know." I explain about Dad and Mom and the cooking situation.

Ms. Raffeli says, "Teddy, I'm asking you to please quiet down."

But now that Lonnie brought up how much I hate lunches, I realize that I don't even know what I've ordered.

"Ms. Raffeli, what is the lunch today?" I ask.

"Teddy, please." Ms. Raffeli is at the front of the class. "We're talking about winning!"

Viva mouths, "Spaghetti and meatballs."

"Oh," I say. The school spaghetti is like eating shoelaces, and the meatballs aren't any better.

"Can I change my order?"

"Teddy, to win the inventors' fair, you need determination, creativity, and focus. I know you've got determination and creativity; please show me you can focus."

"I'm focused," I say. "I'm focused!" And it's sort of true. I'm just focused on the serious mistake I made ordering school lunch.

## GARLIC

When Serena returns, Ms. Raffeli says, "Yesterday, we read about inventors and shared what we learned. Today, we'll learn about the inventor's process. There are four easy steps to creating an invention."

I try really hard not to say anything to Lonnie and Viva about the garlic record, but it's all I can think about. Before I know it I lean over and whisper, "I brought garlic today."

Lonnie looks surprised and whispers back, "Garlic?"

"Teddy," Ms. Raffeli says. "Don't interrupt." She holds up one finger and says, "Step one:

inventors think of a problem."

I wish I could stop myself, but I can't, so I whisper, "To break a record."

"Teddy," Ms. Raffeli says. "Quiet."

"Sorry," I say to Ms. Raffeli. She holds up another finger. "Step two: inventors brainstorm inventions to fix the problem."

I feel like I'm going to explode if I don't tell them about the garlic, but I have to be careful. So I write it on a piece of paper. "Teddy." Ms. Raffeli's eyebrows rise up. "Do you have something to share?"

"Uh, no," I say.

"Then please show me what a winner looks like."

I nod and look straight at her.

"Good," she says. "Step three: inventors choose the best invention."

I slide the paper to Lonnie and Viva. They read it.

"I don't think my mom will let me," Viva whispers.

"I thought you'd say that," I whisper back. "I brought everything to school."

"Teddy, do I have to move you?"

"Sorry."

"Step four: inventors make the invention." Ms. Raffeli looks at me, and when she sees me looking back, she smiles. "Today we'll start with step one. Teddy, can you tell me what step one in the inventor's process is?"

Lewis shouts out, "Brainstorming problems!"

"Please do not shout out, Lewis," Ms. Raffeli says.

Lonnie whispers, "You brought everything to school? Are we're doing it here?"

"At recess!" I say. Unfortunately, I get so excited about this that I actually say it louder than I mean to. By louder, I actually mean like the shouting kind of louder.

Ms. Raffeli says, "Teddy, change seats with Max." Strange but true, the record for tallest man ever is Robert Wadlow, who was 8 feet 11.1 inches. I know I don't have a choice about moving, because Ms. Raffeli's eyebrows are raised so high they could beat that record.

As I sit down at Max's desk, I pull out my to-do list.

I thought breaking a record was hard, but it turns out getting through this list might be harder.

## NEW SEAT, NEW KIDS

Before we go to lunch, Ms. Raffeli takes me aside. "Teddy," she says. "I'm sorry to do this, but I'm going to keep you in your new spot."

"What?" I say. "I thought it was just for today."

"I've reconsidered. This inventors' fair is too important."

"I'll pay attention," I say. "I promise!"

"I think you and Lonnie and Viva need a little time away from each other."

"But Lonnie and Viva haven't moved."

"No, you're right. I should have said you need a little time away from them. They are too tempting, and I need all your attention on this project. I think you'll really like your new seat once we get started."

I nod and head off to lunch, grabbing my backpack on the way out.

## THE FORCE IS WITH US

I try a bite of the spaghetti and meatballs, then put my fork down. I can't believe I'm going to say this, but I wish I had the lunch Dad made.

Lonnie takes a bite of his sandwich. "Don't worry about the seat."

"Yeah," Viva says. "We're still friends wherever we sit."

"And," Lonnie says, "we are breaking a world record. Nothing can come between us and that."

I know they're right, but even if the school lunch tasted wonderful, it would still stick in my throat.

Lonnie says, "So you brought garlic? Enough for us to break the record?"

I nod. My stomach growls.

Viva bites into an apple and says, "And you're thinking we'll do it here? At recess?"

The way they say this makes me wonder if they actually think this is a terrible idea, almost as terrible as the school's spaghetti and meatballs.

Then they smile.

Viva says, "You're a genius."

Lonnie says, "The Force is definitely with you."

And all of a sudden I feel like everything will be okay. I say, "The Force is definitely with us." My stomach growls again.

"You'll need your strength if we're going to do this," Lonnie says. He reaches into his lunch bag and hands me some carrots.

Viva gives me her squeeze yogurt. "We can't have you fainting from hunger in the middle of our record." This is exactly why we're a team. We really know how to take care of each other.

## FAILED RECORD ATTEMPT #6

We manage twelve cloves and then our mouths explode.

I never knew how spicy garlic was. Of course, we don't have any water with us, and the worst part is that the recess monitor won't let us go inside to get any.

Lonnie and Viva resort to eating grass. It seems to help them, so I do it too. That's when the recess monitor tells us we aren't allowed to eat grass.

I admit I've learned a few things from this experience:

1. Eating raw garlic tastes way worse than anyone could ever think.
2. Sometimes grown-ups make up dumb rules like no eating grass.
3. This record was not as easy as I thought it would be.
4. I admire Mom, because she actually does the things on her to-do list. I just dream of doing things.

## WHICH ONE OF YOU IS FARTING?

When we get back to class, I discover that during lunch and recess, Ms. Raffeli moved all my stuff to Max's desk and all his stuff to mine.

I knew she was going to switch us, but it's all more horrible when it's done. It also makes it way harder for me to concentrate on brainstorming inventions, which is what Ms. Raffeli has asked us to do. "Remember," Ms. Raffeli says, "think of a problem in your life and try to solve it with an invention."

My group starts inventing right away. It's amazing how they come up with ideas so quickly.

Ny says, "How about regular shoes that can turn into tap shoes? That way I could tap anywhere and anytime."

"You're a tap dancer?" I ask.

"I knew she was a tap dancer," Lewis says.

Ny stands up and shows me. She's really good. I can see why she'd want tap shoes with her all the time.

"Nice tapping," Lewis says. "Now back to problems. How about glow-in-the-dark baseballs? So you don't lose them at night."

Cornelio says, "How about an electric page turner, so I don't have to turn them?"

Ny says, "That's just lazy."

"I know." Cornelio shrugs. "Sometimes I'm like that."

Serena says, "My only problem is that my hair is so fabulous, people are jealous. But what do you invent to solve that problem?" Serena laughs, but the rest of us are quiet. "I'm joking," she says. And then we all join her.

Unfortunately, I'm not coming up with any ideas, because it turns out that the worst part of trying to break a garlic record is that garlic makes you fart. But the even-worser part is the unbelievable stinkiness of my farts. Who knew garlic farts were so smelly? Considering Edison knew so much about perspiration, you think he'd have invented something to mask really bad stinks.

"Okay," Serena says, "which one of you is farting?"

"That's what I was going to ask," Lewis says.

Cornelio says, "Don't look at me." Which, of course, makes everyone look at him.

I try to hold the farts in, but it's no use. They sneak out. I can see from everyone's face how bad it is. I'm sure the only reason Ms. Raffeli doesn't notice is because she's so busy listening to invention ideas that her nose isn't working.

I can tell that Lonnie and Viva are having the same problem because Max is holding his nose.

Ny says, "It's Teddy."

"That's what I was going to say," Lewis says.

Ny looks at me and says, "How about we make an invention that fights farts?"

Before Lewis can say that he was going to say that, Ny, Serena, and Cornelio burst out laughing. Lewis cracks up too, and I admit, I join them, because it would be a great invention, and honestly my farts are too much even for me.

## HOW COULD I FORGET?

The bell rings, and we're about to rush out when Ms. Raffeli stops us. "Students," she says. "Today is the last day of March, which means tomorrow is April first, also known as April Fools' Day."

"What?" I say.

Ms. Raffeli keeps talking. "In the past there have been jokes played in the classroom. This year there will not be. Instead, we will pour all that creative energy into our inventions!"

I stop listening right there because my brain is taken up with one huge thought: HOW COULD I FORGET APRIL FOOLS' DAY?!!

Lonnie and I love April Fools' Day. It's the best day of the year. We always spend the day before together, planning our pranks.

Max, who is now sitting with Lonnie and Viva, raises his hand. "Ms. Raffeli, I think someone already played a trick. I've been smelling stink bombs all afternoon."

"Is that true?" Ms. Raffeli sniffs. I'm happy to say no one in my group says anything about the stink bombs actually being my farts. Ms. Raffeli grabs her nose and holds it closed, and because she's holding her nose, she can't talk right. "Whoeber led off de stink bombs, I do not want any branks toborrow. Do I bake byself clear?"

For once she's not staring at me.


## THE DAY BEFORE APRIL FOOLS' DAY

"It's a miracle," I say. "An April Fools' Day miracle!" Lonnie and Viva walk into my house. I don't know how they did it, but both of them were allowed to come over today.

Viva says, "Mom figured if I came here, all the tricks would be played on your family, and she'd be safe."

Lonnie smiles. "She doesn't know you very well, does she?"

Viva laughs. "Sometimes I don't think she knows me at all!"

No one in my family is home right now. Mom went to the hardware store with The Destructor and will be gone for an hour. And I know from the calendar on the fridge that all my sisters are busy with activities, which means we won't be interrupted by anyone.

For years Lonnie and I have played pranks together, but this is our first April Fools' Day with Viva. We share with her some of our favorite tricks:

1. Toothpaste on doorknobs.
2. Shaving cream on toilet seats.
3. Switching salt for sugar.
4. Hiding all Dad's underwear under the sofa cushions. (He couldn't find them for hours.)

"My turn!" Viva says.

1. Stuffing newspapers into the toes of shoes.
2. Piling up loads of stuff in the closet so when the door opens, everything falls all over the person who opened the door.
3. Fake candy made from play dough.
4. Tying all the dining room chairs together with fishing line.

Viva says, "I could go on, but you get the idea."
"You've got more?" Lonnie says.
She nods.
For some reason this is not surprising at all.

## UNDERWEAR-GUN DI

When Viva asks why we can't do anything to my sisters, I say, "Trust me. It's not worth the pain they can cause."

Lonnie nods and says, "He's speaking the truth."

Viva says, "What's the point of having siblings if you can't play a prank on them?"

I shake my head. "Your Jedi mind trick won't work on me this time."

"Fine," she says. "But do you have any Oreos? I totally want to try toothpaste Oreos. You scrape the icing filling out and replace it with toothpaste."

Viva knows we always have Oreos. It's Dad's favorite cookie.

"Okay," I agree. "We'll do the Oreo trick on a few cookies and then move on. I only want Dad to eat them."

We probably do more than we mean to, but once we start it's really hard to stop. We hide them in the back of the cabinet so Dad won't find them until tomorrow. Then we move on to the other pranks on our list.

"I've never done newspapers in shoes," I say. So Viva shows us how to ball up sheets of newspaper and shove them into the toes of Mom's and Dad's shoes. We can't tie the chairs together this afternoon because we eat in the dining room every night, but we do find an old pair of binoculars and use some of Sharon's makeup to draw on the eyepiece. Mom and Dad are not birdwatchers, so I'll have to come up with a good excuse for one of them to look through them, but I'll deal with that later. We also collect Dad's underwear to hide in the closet where the cleaning supplies are kept. Viva won't carry any of Dad's underwear because she says it's just gross. We agree with her, but Lonnie stretches the waistband of one pair and shoots it down the stairs. "Watch out, Darth

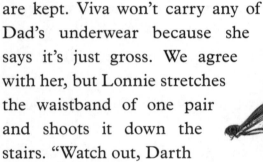

Vader!" he screams. "You're no match against the Jedi Master UNDERWEAR-Gun Di!"

That gets us giggling so much that Lonnie and I drop most of Dad's underpants on the stairs.

## SOMETIMES DOING SOMETHING WRONG IS SO MUCH FUN

That's when Caitlin and Casey walk in. They are sweaty and stinky and clearly have been out collecting trash.

We quickly scoop up the underwear (even Viva!) and shove them into the closet before Caitlin and Casey notice what we're doing. We sit down in the kitchen and try to stifle all the laughs we have in us. It is not easy.

"Hey, Teddy," Caitlin says. "Some kid named Lewis said to say hi."

"We pick up garbage from his family," Caitlin says.

"I'm starving," Casey says.

"Me too," Caitlin says, rummaging in the cabinet.

Caitlin pulls out the Oreos. "Especially after collecting so much trash."

**105**

Casey pauses. "Are you saying you collected more?"

"Do I need to answer that?"

Before I can stop them, they each take a bite. Instantly, their faces change and they spit it out. And instantly we stop laughing.

"Casey, what day is it?" Caitlin says.

"The day before April Fools' Day."

"Funny," they say. "Real funny."

"It wasn't meant for you," Viva says. "We swear."

They put their hands on their hips. "We'll

forgive you this one time," they say. "But don't try it again." And they walk away.

Lonnie, Viva, and I are very quiet until we're sure they're upstairs. Then Lonnie says, "Sometimes doing something wrong is so much fun."

Then we crack up, because it turns out that the day before April Fools' Day is as funny as April Fools' Day.


## HOW TO RUIN A DAY

After Lonnie and Viva leave, I go feed the pigeons. I know The Destructor is still out with Mom, so I'll have the whole place to myself unless Grumpy Pigeon Man comes out, which he does.

"Broken any new records?" he asks.

"Not yet," I say.

"I saw Lonnie and Viva were here. They didn't want to see the pigeons?"

"They couldn't," I say. "Not enough time."

"Of course not. No time for anything except breaking records." He sighs, and it sounds just like our cat, Smarty Pants, when she sneezes.

"I'm back!" The Destructor crashes through

the door. The pigeons flutter around. Of course Grumpy Pigeon Man doesn't tell him to be quiet.

The Destructor holds out his hand. "Want one?" he asks Grumpy Pigeon Man. He's carrying a bunch of Oreos. "Mom said I should share."

"How thoughtful," Grumpy Pigeon Man says.

"Where'd you get those?"

"From the house, of course!"

I know I should say something, but my April Fools' Day brain stops me. I watch them bite into the toothpaste Oreos, waiting for a reaction.

"Yummy," The Destructor says.

"Is this a new flavor? It's so minty," Grumpy Pigeon Man says.

I walk back to the house and leave them with

their cookies. Those two really know how to ruin April Fools' Day.

## MY FAVORITE INVENTIONS

When I walk back into the kitchen I grab the book Ms. Raffeli gave me for homework and settle down to start reading. My book is all about African American inventors. Ms. Raffeli told us to write up three facts, but this book is so great I've already found four, and I'm only halfway through!

So far these are my favorite inventors and their inventions:

1. George Crum: inventor of the potato chip. (I love potato chips.)
2. Marie Van Brittan Brown: inventor of the first home security system. (I wish I had one to warn me when The Destructor is in the aviary.)
3. Garrett Morgan: inventor of the traffic signal. (Sometimes I think we could use a traffic signal in our house—especially concerning the bathroom.)
4. Lonnie G. Johnson: inventor of the Super

Soaker squirt gun. (The best water pistol ever—Lonnie will love this!)

## SURPRISE

I'm still reading about inventors when Grace walks into the kitchen. I know my feet are safe from her because I have them tucked under the table right next to The Destructor, who has made another nest.

She surprises me by hitting me in the head with a rolled-up newspaper and then tossing it in front of me. It's her school newspaper. Right there on the very front page is a picture of my tent and me! The headline reads: *Teddy Mars: World Record Breaker!* "I still can't believe they wanted this story," Grace says. "Where's the news in this? It's old. It's boring. And it's about *you*!"

I have to say, I agree with her. Why would the middle school newspaper want a story about me sleeping in a tent longer than anyone else my age? Then I start reading the article, and it's like I'm reading about someone else. It's actually interesting.

Grace walks over to the cabinet to look for a snack. "Now they want another story," she says. "But they've rejected all my ideas. I don't know what I'm going to do. I have to be known for something more than my nut-o brother." She digs around, clearly not happy with what she sees. "Mom needs to buy some better snacks." She reaches and pulls out the Oreos.

Before I can explain that those are for Dad, she pops one in her mouth. Her face collapses. "Blech!" She sticks out her tongue and wipes it with her hand.

The Destructor sticks his head out from under the table. "If you're not going to finish that, I will."

Grace backs me into a corner. "Very funny," she says.

"They weren't for you," I say.

Grace slams on my foot and walks away.

"Gosh," The Destructor says. "I guess she doesn't like those cookies." He scoots back into his nest and I'm left cradling my foot and remembering how dangerous April Fools' Day can be.

And it's not even April Fools' Day yet!

## APRIL FOOLS' DAY

I wake up to The Destructor jumping up and down on my stomach like he's breaking the record for most seat drops on a trampoline (49 in one minute).

"Wake up! Wake up! Wake up!" he hollers.

I leap out of bed. "What time is it?"

"April Fools' Day!" he shouts. I look at my clock and it's four in the morning. An hour and a half before I normally wake up. Everyone else is still asleep.

"What is wrong with you?" I ask.

"It's April Fools' Day. I didn't want you to miss it."

"Thanks," I say. I crawl back into bed. I'm pretty much wide awake, and so is The Destructor, who is climbing into his pigeon costume.

"I'm going out to the birds. You want to come?"

"It's a little early, isn't it?" I ask.

"It's never too early for the birds. First one there's the winner!" he says, and runs out of our room.

I scramble out of bed.

Considering how short his legs are, he is fast, but I fly down the stairs and pass him at the front door.

The Destructor will not beat me to the aviary.

## NEVER

The Destructor is only a few seconds behind me. But I still get there first, which means I am the winner. Unlike me, who starts work as soon as I walk into the aviary, The Destructor immediately sits down on a bucket and stares at the pigeons.

While I'm outside filling up the water bucket, Grumpy Pigeon Man shuffles out of his house. "What in the name of pigeon is going on here? Is this some kind of joke? You're early! And in your pajamas!"

I'm too tired to explain. I carry the bucket into the loft, the screened-in part of the aviary. Grumpy Pigeon Man follows me. "Oh, I see Pigeon Boy is here."

The Destructor waves to Grumpy Pigeon Man, who sits down next to him.

I'm timing the birds, because they are only allowed to eat for ten minutes, and then I have to take the food away. I guess if the food was left out, pigeons would just keep eating until they got sick. I'm counting seconds in my head because I don't have a watch.

Grumpy Pigeon Man says, "Do you see those birds?" He's talking to The Destructor, but I can't help looking over. He points to four birds huddled together on a perch. I know those birds. Lonnie, Viva, and I named them: Obi-Wan Kenobi, Stass Allie, Yoda, and Ima-Gun Di. He says, "I got those birds from a one-eyed sailor."

"Really?" The Destructor says. I start to ask if that's true but stop, because I remember he isn't talking to me.

"Would I lie to you?" Grumpy Pigeon Man says. "I was a sailor, and a shipmate of mine kept these pigeons."

"Sailors are supposed to have parrots," The Destructor says.

"What kind of sailor would want a parrot on a ship?" Grumpy Pigeon Man shakes his head. "Too noisy. And the pigeons can carry messages. Attach a note to its foot and let it go. Pigeons are the mail carriers of the skies. Parrots can't do that."

I admit it is very hard to know if Grumpy Pigeon Man is making up this story or not. It's also hard to watch him being so nice to The Destructor when all he does is grump at me. And right then he says, "Tent Boy, ten minutes is up. Get on with your work, or Pigeon Boy will do it for you."

I jump to it, moving quickly to take the food away. The Destructor may get the good stories, but he will never have my job.

Never.

## ★ MY TO-DO LIST #7 ★

Mom's making breakfast for me when The Destructor comes back home. He's yakking to Mom all about Grumpy Pigeon Man. To block out the noise I pull out my list. It's already so messy it's hard to read. I get a clean piece of paper and start a new one. It's satisfying to start a new list, but totally disappointing that nothing ever changes on it.

1. Invent a way to keep The Destructor far from me.
2. Invent a way to keep The Destructor out of the aviary.
3. Break a world record with Lonnie and Viva.
4. Get my old desk back.

That's when I bite into the toast Mom made for me. I start to gag.

"April Fools'!" she screams.

"What's on it?"

"Elmer's glue! I put Elmer's glue on instead of butter!" She's bent over laughing. Only Mom could get away with this. "What's the matter? You used to eat glue all the time in kindergarten and you turned out just fine."

"Funny, Mom. Very funny!" I say. I have to admit, it might be the best prank ever, and I know it took her years to think of because she's never played a prank on me before. Maybe it's the same with my list. I just need to give myself more time.

Hopefully not as long as Mom needed; that would just be annoying.

## BIGGER THAN UNDERPANTS

I'm in line for school with Lonnie and Viva. Lonnie is doubled over with laughter. "Tell me again," he says between breaths.

Viva has fallen down on the blacktop from laughing so hard. "It's fall-down funny!" she blurts out.

I tell them again. "Mom put Elmer's glue on my toast. But what you should really be laughing about is that I got her to look through the binoculars and she ended up with dark circles all around her eyes. Then she rubbed her eyes, so the black makeup spread all over her face. Dad couldn't find his underwear, which was hilarious until he screamed at me that he needed to get to work. When he tried to slip on his shoes he couldn't. And because The Destructor woke me so early, I managed to tie the chairs together before anyone came downstairs. That'll be the big surprise for tonight."

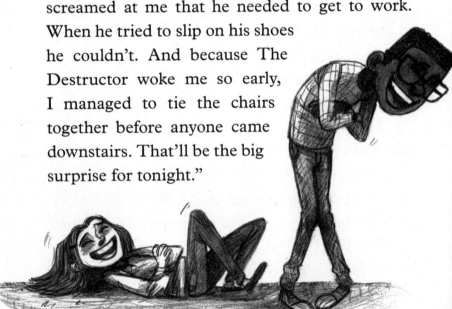

Viva stands up. "Oh, my cheeks hurt from laughing so hard."

"Tell me about it," Lonnie says, clutching his stomach. "But what about the cookies?"

"I don't think there are any left," I say. "But I'm not sure." They know about Caitlin and Casey, but I explain about The Destructor and Grumpy Pigeon Man and then about Grace.

At which point, Viva falls down on the ground again.

"Do you even remember how many we made?" I ask.

None of us can remember. "Well, after the glue toast I had for breakfast, I am not tasting the cookies to find out."

I take a moment more to appreciate April Fools' Day, and then I change the subject. "And now, back to business. What record can we break?"

Lonnie says, "How about the most baking sheets buckled over the head in one minute?"

"Really?" Viva says.

"I think it looks cool, and I don't think it would hurt," Lonnie says. "The picture makes it look fun. One person bashes the baking sheet over the other person's head."

"Oh brother," Viva says. "Isn't there any record

my mom wouldn't mind?"

"I doubt it," Lonnie says.

Right then Lewis runs straight into me. "I knew it! I knew you did something big! Why didn't you tell anyone?"

"Tell anyone about what?" I ask.

"You know how I'm always first in line, except for today and a couple of days ago? Well, I'm late today because I've been reading the newspaper my sister brought home from middle school. And look who's on the front page!" He shoves the paper into Lonnie's and Viva's faces. "You broke a world record!" he yells. I have to admit, I forgot all about the article Grace wrote. The whole class, and maybe some kids in the other classes, turns around.

And there's a silence that makes me feel like I have been caught wearing the world's biggest pair of underpants (65 feet 7 inches by 39 feet 4 inches). That's bigger than three giraffes stacked on top of each other.

Those are *big* underpants.


## IT'S THE TRUTH

Ny breaks the silence and says, "Is this an April Fools' Day joke?"

"That's what I thought," Lewis says. "But no. It's actually true."

"What record?" Cornelio says.

"Teddy slept in a tent longer than any other kid ever!"

Angus hops over and says, "In a tent?"

"I don't believe it," Serena says, flipping her hair and whacking me in the face.

"Here's the proof," Lewis says, holding it out for everyone to see.

"You didn't tell me you were in the paper," Lonnie says. I explain about Grace and her new job as a reporter and how she was forced into it.

"That's a long time to sleep in a tent," Ny says. "I tried to chew gum for the longest time, but after four hours my jaw hurt so much I had to stop."

Lewis says, "I've always wanted to break a record." I have to admit, this is surprising. Lewis is so clean.

"How did you even see the paper?" I ask.

"I told you," Lewis says. "My sister goes to the middle school. She runs track with your sister."

I didn't even know Lewis had a sister. I wonder how he knows so much about mine.

"Can I have your autograph?" Angus says.

"Why haven't you been on TV?" Lewis says.

"If I broke a record I'd be on TV."

Cornelio says, "Or in the real newspaper."

I start to stammer out an answer, but Lonnie says, "If you knew his family, you'd know it's a miracle that they even got him into *The Guinness Book of World Records*."

Viva nods. "There are a lot of Mars kids to take care of."

I have to admit, it's really nice to have friends who know me so well that I don't have to explain everything all by myself.

## THE GOLDEN POISON DART FROG

We're all filing into school when Lewis runs up to Ms. Raffeli and shows her the paper.

"How could I have forgotten about your record?" Ms. Raffeli says. "It is really something!"

"You have a lot on your mind right now," I say.

"That's true," she says. "And because of that, we really don't want to waste a minute."

When we get to our desks Lewis says, "Call him Tent Boy. That's what his sister calls him in the article, and that is an awesome nickname." He raises his hand for me to give him a high five. I look over at Lonnie and Viva's cluster, where I don't sit anymore, and their eyes get all big. They know how much I hate that name.

"Lewis," Ms. Raffeli says.

"Sorry, Ms. Raffeli." Lewis has this way of saying sorry that makes everyone believe him. Then he whispers, "We have got to break a record together, Tent Boy."

I'm about to tell him that Lonnie, Viva, and I are already breaking a record, but he interrupts and says, "It's going to be awesome, Tent Boy. Just awesome."

And that's when Ms. Raffeli says, "Teddy, do I have to move you again?"

And I decide not to say a word, because moving once was bad enough.

Strange but true, the most venomous frog is the golden poison dart frog. Moving again would be like being bitten by one of those. I probably wouldn't survive.

## CRAB SOCCER

I can't be the only one who thinks it's weird that Lewis picked me for his team in gym class. He never picks me for his team.

In fact, I know I'm not the only one who thinks it's weird, because Lonnie and Viva are staring at me like I'm the largest cockroach in the world (3.8 inches long by 1.75 inches wide), which is just gross.

And even though I find Lewis a little annoying, it's strangely satisfying to be winning at crab soccer. It's totally a first for me.

Unfortunately, Lonnie and Viva are on the other team, and they don't look so happy.

## THE FIRST TIME IN HISTORY

Strange but true, there are a lot of firsts in history, and it's amazing to think that most of them happened because of an invention.

1. The first flushing toilet was invented around 2500 BCE in the Indus Valley. (Cornelio says that's where parts of Pakistan, Afghanistan, and India are now.)
2. The first eyeglasses were invented about 1286.
3. The first safety pin was invented in 1849.

All these are quite mind-boggling when you really think about them. But the most incredible first is the first time in the history of eating lunch at our school that other kids sit with Lonnie, Viva, and me.

Today, our table is packed. Lewis, Cornelio, Ny, Serena, Angus, and the two Jasmines are sitting with us, which means there is barely enough room to bend my elbow and get my food into my mouth. And they ask me a million questions about sleeping in the tent.

I can tell by the look on Lonnie's and Viva's faces that it's as overwhelming for them as it is for me. I felt the same when I first read about the person who ate 200 worms in 30 seconds. I wondered, is this true? And then I wondered, what was the person thinking? And then I wondered, how do you even manage to swallow one live worm?

I mean, 200 worms is a lot of worms.

## EASIEST HOMEWORK EVER

During recess, Lonnie, Viva, and I slip away. There's only so much attention a person can stand. But once we're back in the classroom, Lewis keeps asking me where we were. And what record we should break. Finally, I say, "Lewis, I'm really trying to listen."

Which is definitely the first time I have ever said anything like that. Ms. Raffeli looks over at

126

me and smiles, and that's a really great feeling.

Ms. Raffeli says, "We've already spent time in class brainstorming inventions. For tonight's homework, I want each of you to think up *three* inventions to share with your group. Tomorrow your group will pick one of those to make for the inventors' fair.

And please bring in any recyclables, fabric, nails, hammers—anything from home that we might use to build our inventions. Get a good night's sleep, because from here on out, school is getting serious."

This is the easiest homework ever.

1. Thinking up crazy ideas is something I've got a lot of practice in, thanks to *The Guinness Book of World Records*. So that'll be easy.
2. I don't have to look for anything to bring in because Mom and Dad don't save any-thing. My family is so huge, they say that if they kept everything we brought into the house, there would be no room for us.
3. I never have a hard time sleeping.

## A LITTLE HARDER

What I am not prepared for is the sudden sinking feeling I get when I remember that I am no longer in Lonnie and Viva's group. We won't be making an invention together. Then I see Lonnie, Viva, and Max all make a plan to meet after school so they can go over their invention ideas.

The record for hardest secret code to crack is from World War II. The United States used the Navajo language, as well as a few other things that I don't understand, to write secret messages for their allies. Eight hundred messages were sent over two days, and not a single one was figured out by the enemy.

That's how hard the code was to break.

Right now my life feels a little harder than that code.


## EVEN HARDER

When I get home, I skip snack and start right away on my homework. I have to say, coming up with inventions is harder than I thought it would be, because all the inventions I think of are too hard to make.

For example:

1. A chocolate bar that will never melt.
2. Band-Aids that don't hurt when you rip them off. (Mom says they exist and that she even buys them, but I don't believe her.)
3. Cars that run on poop, because that's something we'll always have.

I'd like to blame all my troubles on my family, who are louder than the 1,361 accordions that broke the record for most accordions played at one time. I'm not sure I know what one accordion sounds like, but 1,361 of any musical instrument has got to be loud.

But I know there's another reason I'm not thinking of a good invention, and that is because I'm not in the same group as Lonnie and Viva.

That makes everything even harder.

## ★ MY TO-DO LIST #8 ★

1. Invent a way to keep The Destructor far from me.
2. Invent a way to keep The Destructor out of the aviary.
3. Break a world record with Lonnie and Viva.

4.  Get my old desk back.
5.  Come up with an invention.

## GRUMPY PIGEON MAN
## AND HIS INVENTIONS

In the end, I go out to the aviary. Of course, The Destructor and Grumpy Pigeon Man are here, but it's still my favorite place to think.

Grumpy Pigeon Man and The Destructor are sitting on the only two buckets. So, as usual, I stand.

Grumpy Pigeon Man points to Chewbacca and Han Solo. "Those two birds there—those two came from a train engineer."

"Really?" The Destructor says.

Grumpy Pigeon Man nods. "I worked for the

railroad for a time. Fixing the trains. There was an engineer who wanted company while he drove the train, so he got the two pigeons. It turned out he wasn't allowed to keep them in the engine car. So I got them. Those two might be the only pigeons in the world to travel by train."

"Wow," The Destructor says.

I'd say wow too, and not because of the story. I've never heard Grumpy Pigeon Man talk this much before.

Grumpy Pigeon Man turns to me. "What are you doing, Tent Boy? You know I don't pay you to sit around."

"I'm not sitting around," I say. "First of all, I'm standing, and second of all, I'm thinking."

"Well, hop to it." He hands me the pigeons' bowl. "Those pigeons can't feed themselves."

"You can't put a timer on thinking, sir." I take the bowl. "It's homework."

I'm about to walk out and get seed for the pigeons, but Grumpy Pigeon Man says, "Your homework is thinking? What kind of crazy homework is that? In my day we filled in worksheets."

"I have to think of an invention."

"Invention?" he grumps. "You don't think up

inventions by sitting around. You think of inventions by doing things."

He turns to The Destructor and says, "I invented something once: the Automatic Pigeon Feeder. I hooked it up to my house. The whole contraption fed and watered them, and I never had to leave my kitchen."

"Why did you stop using it?" I ask.

"Why create an invention that keeps me away from these birds? Stupidest thing I ever made. Now, go feed the pigeons."

I do what he says, even though it isn't actually time for their dinner, but I figure the chances of me coming up with any inventions right now are as good as me pogo sticking underwater for 1,580 feet.

It's not going to happen.

## GRUMPY PIGEON MAN WAS WRONG

That night another first happens: I can't sleep.

I'm pretty sure everyone in the house is already asleep, but it's a little hard to tell since

The Destructor is snoring so loudly.

I worked on my ideas all afternoon, but I haven't come up with an invention. I flip through *The Guinness Book of World Records* hoping maybe it will inspire me. All it does is remind me that Lonnie, Viva, and I have not broken a record yet.

Because I can't sleep, I decide to go out to the aviary. I sneak past everyone's bedroom and stop in the kitchen to write a note for Mom explaining where I am.

In the aviary, I sit on a bucket and look around. The pigeons' heads are tucked into the feathers, or else they are just nestled down—their bodies plumped up. All of them are asleep except Admiral Ackbar, who's looking at me like I'm the enemy. But because he doesn't actually attack me, I'm not worried.

There's something so cozy and warm about the aviary. My eyes begin to close, my head slowly hangs down, and then suddenly I jerk awake. A minute later, it's happening again. I'm feeling so tired I hold up my head with my hand.

That's when I think of it! My invention!

A portable pillow shaped like my arm and hand that would hold my head up when I'm tired.

I guess Grumpy Pigeon Man was wrong. Sometimes all you have to do is just sit around and you will think up an invention.


## A HISTORIC EVENT

I wake up on the sofa with my notepad next to me. Mom says, "Teddy? What are you doing down here? I thought you'd be out feeding the pigeons with Jake."

"The pigeons! What time is it?" I look at the clock and see that I'm an hour late. "The Destructor is already out there?"

Mom nods. "He woke me up and said he was going."

"The sneak," I say under my breath so Mom can't hear. I don't have a lot of time to get ready for school, so I have to let it go. But I can't make the same mistake again tomorrow.

I'm happy to report, though, that because of Caitlin and Casey's trash business, I actually have recycled stuff to bring to school (another first in my life). Mom even drives me, not only because I'm late, but also because of the three trash bags. One bag is full of cardboard, newspapers, and plastic tubs. The other two are full of plastic bags. I guess a lot of people recycle the plastic bags they get from the grocery store.

We drive up to the school drop-off loop. Mom helps get the bags out, but the cars behind her honk, so I have to lug them into school myself. My class is already lined up; Lewis is first, right where he likes to be. Lonnie and Viva are in the middle in a deep conversation with Max. I'm dragging two bags on the ground and one is slung over my back like Santa's sack.

"Tent Boy?" I look up and Lewis runs up to me. He hoists a bag over his shoulder, and then helps with the one I'm dragging. Carrying them is way easier with someone else. I really appreciate it. And on top of that, Lewis actually left his spot to help me. "Wow," Lewis says. "You brought a lot. Is this all from Caitlin and Casey?"

"Yeah," I say.

"Your family is different from normal families," he says.

"I hear that a lot."

"You know I meant it about breaking a world record," Lewis says. "I've got a lot of ideas. I like those records where a bunch of people do the same thing at one time."

"You mean group records?" I say with a gulp. I still hate group records.

He nods. "They're so cool."

"There are loads of other great records to break," I say.

"Like what?" Lewis says.

Of course, I can't think of any at that very second, and when we make it to our line, everyone circles around us.

"What's in the bags?" Lonnie asks.

I open them so they can see what I've brought.

"That's a lot of plastic bags," Viva says. "What are you going to do with them all?"

I shrug. "I'm just happy I have something to share."

Lonnie laughs. "Seriously, this day will go down in the history books. I might even make it a holiday."

Viva claps and yells, "Speech! Speech!"

I'm not much of a speechmaker, so I just take a bow.

## LONGEST DAY

The longest time anyone held his breath under water is 22 minutes. That's long! I'm sorry to say that today feels longer, and I've only been at school for ten minutes.

I thought Ms. Raffeli would switch me back to my old seat when she saw how many recyclables I'd brought in. But when I ask her, she says, "Teddy, you're doing very well where you are."

I say, "So I'm staying where I am?"

She nods.

"For the rest of the year?"

She nods.

"But I can be on Lonnie and Viva's invention team, right?"

She shakes her head no and says, "I want you

inventing with the group you sit with."

I open my mouth to complain, but her eyebrows fly up. And just like I know that the world record for smelling the most feet (5,600) must be the stinkiest way to break a record, I also know that there's no use in arguing with my teacher. Neither Ms. Raffeli nor her eyebrows are budging.

### ★ MY TO-DO LIST #9 ★

1. Invent a way to keep The Destructor far from me.
2. Invent a way to keep The Destructor out of the aviary.
3. Break a world record with Lonnie and Viva.
4. ~~Get my old desk back.~~
5. ~~Come up with an invention.~~
6. Muddle through school for the rest of the year.

## AS BIG AS THAT

I look around the room and at the clusters of desks, which are *now* our four invention teams.

Team #1: Philip, Nick, Bekka, and Alanis

Team #2: Angus, Jasmine B., Jasmine H., and Chrystal

Team #3: Lonnie, Viva, and Max

Team #4: Lewis, Ny, Cornelio, Serena, and me

As I think about these teams, it suddenly dawns on me that we're not only competing against the other fourth-grade classes, but we're competing against each other. Which means some of us will win, but others will lose.

I've never really thought about winning before. Breaking a record was always just something I wanted to do. But now that I've come up with an invention of my own, winning the inventors' fair seems kind of cool. Except me winning means beating my two best friends. And maybe they should win, since they haven't broken a record, yet.

And then Ms. Raffeli says, "Serena, I want you to move your desk to sit with Lonnie, Viva, and Max. That will make the numbers more even."

I can't believe it. I should be the one with working with Lonnie and Viva. It's just so wrong. How can Ms. Raffeli do this to me? When I look over at them, they're giving Serena high fives.

Strange but true, the record for the largest desert in the world is the Sahara. At this very moment, I feel like the space between them and me is that big, but they don't seem to notice.

## DRAWING YODA

We've begun sharing our inventions with our teams. Since I only have the one idea for the head holder, I'm done pretty quickly.

Lewis shakes his head. "So, you can break a record, but you can only come up with one invention?" He looks a little worried, and soon I understand why. It's because every one of them has thought up at least five ideas each. Ms. Raffeli says we have to get our list down to one invention per person, and then out of those she'll decide on the invention we'll make.

All their ideas are fabulous, and it's hard to pick just one. For a little while, making decisions is fun. What's better, a bubble suit that lets you bang into walls and not get hurt, or an umbrella that you don't need your hands to hold? Or a swimsuit that inflates into a life raft?

And those are just Ny's ideas.

Lewis begins sharing his. The first one is pretty

interesting. He calls it a Doggy-Doo Collector. It's a thingamajig you attach to your dog that catches its poo in a plastic bag, so all you have to do is tie up the bag. I love this idea, but I admit, after this one I stop paying attention. Maybe it's because I look over at Lonnie, Viva, Max, and now Serena. They were the first to hand in their list to Ms. Raffeli and are now allowed to do free drawing until lunch.

I pretend I need to sharpen my pencil and as I walk past Lonnie I tap him on the shoulder. But he's too wrapped up in his drawing of Yoda to look up. I want to ask him what his invention idea is. Viva doesn't look up either. She's drawing Yoda, too. Actually now that I look more carefully I realize that they are all drawing Yoda. Even Max and Serena. Finally Lonnie sees me. "We're having a Yoda-off to see who can draw the best Yoda."

I nod and slip back into my new desk, wishing I was drawing Yoda, too.

## ★ MY TO-DO LIST #10 ★

Lunch is a repeat of yesterday. Lonnie, Viva, and I are surrounded and have no time by ourselves. Lonnie and Viva are talking to Max about world records. "If I were to break a record I'd do a collection," Max says. "I already have twenty-five different kinds of rubber bands."

"Rubber bands?" Lonnie asks.

Viva says, "How different can rubber bands be?"

Max says, "Oh, really different! There are variations in color, size, and where they're made."

"I still like those group records," Lewis says. "Did you know there's a record for most people playing the game paper, rock, scissors at the same time?"

Jasmine B. says, "I love that game."

Jasmine H. says, "Me too."

"How do you play it?" Ny asks.

Lewis starts to show her, and pretty soon everyone at the table is playing. Even Lonnie and Viva.

Lunch is starting to feel like my home: too loud, too crowded.

I take out my list and revise it, again.

1. Invent a way to keep The Destructor far from me.
2. Invent a way to keep The Destructor out of the aviary.
3. Break a world record with Lonnie and Viva.
4. ~~Get my old desk back.~~
5. ~~Come up with an invention.~~
6. Muddle through school for the rest of the year.
7. Have three seconds alone with Lonnie and Viva.

## AT LONG LAST

Usually Lonnie, Viva, and I hang out by the swings. We always have a lot to talk about: Star Wars, pigeons, *The Guinness Book of World Records*. But today right after lunch Lewis drags them away to play tag. I don't know how he does it, but every recess Lewis organizes just about every fourth grader into some kind of game—every fourth grader except Lonnie, Viva, and me. Except today, when they join the game right away.

"Come on, Tent Boy," Lewis shouts. "You have to play too!" At first I'm not sure. It feels a little close to a group record, but I don't have anything else to do since Lonnie and Viva are dashing around. So I join the game.

Lewis runs up and says, "We should totally break a record for the most people playing tag."

Luckily, I'm panting too much to answer, but it makes me worried that he's really going to try a group record and I'll be forced to do it with him.

I pause to catch my breath and Ny runs up and tags me. "You're it!" she shouts, so I start chasing. It's actually fun and quite nice to think about

something else besides how I'm not sitting with Lonnie and Viva.

So at long last, time finally goes faster than it has all day, and the only bummer is that recess is only twenty minutes long.


## REMARKABLE

Back in the classroom, everyone is pretty wiggly, and of course, Angus is hoppy. Ms. Raffeli claps her hands and we quiet down so she can tell us what inventions we'll be making.

"Team number one," she says. "Philip, Nick, Bekka, and Alanis will make the Go Kid Go Wagon. A new way to get to around powered by a crank." Ms. Raffeli looks up at their group and nods. "Transportation is always a popular theme in the inventors' fair."

We give them a round of applause.

"Team number two is Angus, Jasmine B., Jasmine H., and Chrystal. They will invent a musical baby blanket."

Angus smiles and says, "And it's all thanks to my new baby brother, who only sleeps when there's music playing!"

Ms. Raffeli explains that anything to do with

**145**

babies wins over the kids in the school.

"And now." Ms. Raffeli smiles. "Team number three, Lonnie, Viva, Max, and Serena, will make a battery-operated trash compactor. We all want our trash to take up less space, and green inventions are very in."

We clap for them. Lonnie stands up and takes a bow.

"And, last but not least, team number four, Lewis, Ny, Cornelio, and Teddy."

Finally, it's our invention. I cross my fingers. I really hope she picks my head holder.

Ms. Raffeli says, "You'll be inventing—"

I hold my breath.

"The Doggy-Doo Collector!"

I admit, I'm very surprised, because doggy doo is not the sort of thing Ms. Raffeli is usually interested in. But she says that any invention that has to do with animals is always a hit!

Then I wonder, Would I rather work on the

Doggy-Doo Collector or the battery-operated trash compacter? And I get the biggest surprise of all! I realize that I'd pick the Doggy-Doo Collector any day, even if it means not working with Lonnie and Viva.

This is remarkably surprising to me and makes me feel like a traitor.


## PSSST! PSSST!

Ms. Raffeli has asked all the groups to draw up a detailed sketch of the invention we're making. She walks around the room helping teams. Angus is singing at the top of his voice to his team. "Rock-a-by baaaby in the treeeeetop!" Listening to Angus sing makes me realize how good Sharon actually is.

"Angus," Ms. Raffeli says, "let's wait on picking the song and start with what you'll need to make it."

Our group is drawing out Lewis's idea. Cornelio draws a stick dog, and Lewis says, "So we want some contraption that will hold a bag under the dog and catch its poo."

I look over at all the plastic bags I brought in. "We've got a lot of those."

Lewis keeps talking about how to attach the bag to the dog. I hear everything he's saying, but only halfway, because I'm staring at all the plastic bags I brought in.

It's as if it's the first time I've actually seen them, and now plastic bags are taking over my brain. Suddenly, I get all tingly and zippy thinking about those plastic bags and how Viva won't get sick or be hurt by them!

It takes all my willpower not to tell Lonnie and Viva my idea. I have to wait until the end of the day. I don't want anyone to get in trouble because of me.

But every time I think about my idea, my heart gets all poundy, and my skin gets squirmy, which makes no sense at all except that it's how I feel.

I keep looking at the clock, which is still going super slowly today. We have an hour left of school.

"Psst, psst, psst!"

I look over at Viva, who is the one making the *psst* noises.

Lonnie waves me over.

I check to make sure the coast is clear. Ms. Raffeli is with Ny's group, so I sneak to Lonnie and Viva's.

"We've come up with a record to break," Lonnie whispers.

"No way," I say. "So did I."

"You're not supposed to be talking," Serena says.

"If you don't interrupt we'll be done in a second," Viva says. "Teddy, you go first."

"No," I say. "You go first."

Lonnie pauses and looks around to be sure Ms. Raffeli is still busy. Then he says, "The largest collection of plastic bags."

I could fall over right there and then, because that is exactly the same thing I was going to say.

"That was my idea, too!"

Max says, "I think my collection of rubber bands was an inspiration."

"Teddy?" Ms. Raffeli is looking straight at me. "Get back to your group."

Lonnie and Viva give a thumbs-up as I walk away.

Things are definitely looking up. And even though Ms. Raffeli sounded mad, I've still got the exciting feeling zipping through my body.

## PSSST! PSSST! PART 2

I sit down because I'm supposed to, but I'd actually like to be hopping around like Angus is doing right now. I look over at the picture Cornelio has drawn, and it looks really good—not at all like a stick dog anymore. We'll have things to figure out, but it's stuff we can do. I have to admit, between breaking a record and this inventors' fair, life couldn't get any better!

Lewis leans over and says, "I've been thinking about a record to break."

"Really?" I say. I'm sure he's going to suggest a group record. This time I'll have to be honest and explain my feeling about group records.

"I'm dying to break a record," Ny says.

Lewis says, "I've got a genius idea. You're going to love it. And no one has thought of it yet."

Cornelio says, "Spit it out."

Lewis says, "We could totally break the record for the largest collection of plastic bags."

This time I do fall over. It's just too weird.

"Teddy!" Ms. Raffeli snaps. "Sit in your chair!"

I do what she says, and I don't say a thing, because even though I still can't believe I feel this way, I really don't want to move my seat again.

## IT'S NOT A COMPETITION

As we walk out of school that day I'm curious how everyone will feel as I explain how we all came up with the same idea about breaking a record.

Lonnie, Viva, and Lewis all freeze on the spot.

"What are we going to do?" Lewis says. "We can't all break the same record."

"I thought you loved group records," I say.

"But this isn't a group record. This is the most-plastic-bags-collected record."

"We thought of it first," Viva says.

"You can't prove that," Lewis says.

"We've been trying to break a record for longer," Viva says.

Lewis says, "Why does that matter?"

I guess this answers how they feel. They don't like it.

"Stop," Lonnie says, and he smiles. "It's not a competition. We can all do it together."

"But," I ask, "will that make it a group record?"

Lonnie rolls his eyes. "No, Teddy," he says. "We're going for most bags collected, not the most people to collect bags."

"Right," I say. "I knew that."

"If Lonnie says we should do it together, I'll

do it together," Viva agrees.

"That's what I was going to say," Lewis says.

Viva looks at Lewis. "You have got to stop saying that." And then she laughs and says, "Just kidding." And then everyone laughs, including Lewis.

And I have to admit, this is the first time in my life I've ever actually been on a team, and suddenly I'm on two. So far it's very cool.


## THE BIG RED CIRCLE

Viva whips out a calendar from her backpack. "My mom makes me carry one so I know what's going on."

She scans the calendar and then points. "The inventors' fair is on a Friday. How about we break the record the next day?"

We circle around her and look.

Lonnie says, "That gives us about a month."

"That's what I was going to say," Lewis says.

Viva stops and stares at him.

"What did I do?" Lewis says.

Viva sighs, pulls out a red marker, and draws a big red circle around that Saturday. "This is going to be awesome!"

"Nothing will stop us!" Lonnie says.

Lewis raises his hand and we do a whole group high five.

Then Ny, Serena, and Max run onto their bus before it takes off.

I grab Viva's calendar and look at the big red circle.

I've only been part of this team for about a minute, but for the second time in that minute, I'm amazed by how cool it is.

## HOME IS GETTING CRAZIER

I thought school days were crazy, but this weekend just broke that record. Mom and Dad are drawing up a chart to compare the jobs they do around the house.

Sharon is not answering Jerome's phone calls because he got a bigger part in the musical than she did. (I know this because the house phone keeps ringing and ringing.)

Caitlin and Casey are fighting over who collects the most trash. Caitlin is in the lead. (At least from the scales' point of view.)

Maggie is freaking out that she lost another race to Bella Colon, even if it was only by one fifth of a second. (I don't even know what a one fifth of a second is.)

Grace tried to stomp on my foot, but I picked it up before she could. (Unfortunately, she stomped on the other one.)

The Destructor is in the aviary holding Admiral Ackbar and listening to more stories about how Grumpy Pigeon Man got his pigeons.

My family has never been normal. But this seems overboard even for them.

## IT'S TIME

As I get up Monday morning, The Destructor jumps out of bed. I race to get my clothes on first while The Destructor struggles with his Pigeon

Boy costume. I don't wait around but run down the stairs and out to the aviary.

I hear his feet behind me as I grab the bucket to fill with water.

He runs up to me, panting. "You sure are fast," he says. "I don't know how you're so fast. Can I help with that bucket?"

"No," I say.

He shrugs and  wanders into the aviary, and I struggle with the bucket now filled with water. When I get there, The Destructor is pouring the pigeon food into their food container.

"What are you doing?" I say.

"I'm feeding the pigeons. Mr. Marney taught me how."

"It's not that easy. We have to time it," I say as the pigeons flock around, grabbing the seeds that

The Destructor has poured.

"I know," he says. "I've got a watch." He sticks his hand into my face, pulls up his sleeve, and shows me.

"Where'd you get that from?" I ask.

"Mr. Marney gave it to me. He said if I was going to take care of the pigeons I better have a watch. It even has an alarm so I know when ten minutes is up." The Destructor presses some buttons and the watch beeps. "See?" he says. He presses another button and it stops.

Grumpy Pigeon Man gave him a watch! He's never given me anything except a lot of hollering! (And, of course, a sleeping bag when I lived in my tent—but that doesn't count. If I'd frozen to death, I wouldn't have been able to take care of his pigeons.)

If I knew the pigeons wouldn't get scared, I would scream my head off!

Instead I storm back to the house, trying to think up ways to destroy The Destructor. Unfortunately, I'm so mad I don't come up with any.

But, like Thomas Edison, I'm going to give it one more try.

## STARTING NOW

I was so distracted by The Destructor this morning that I forgot to bring any plastic bags to school. I actually don't even remember until I see Lonnie and Viva walk up together, pulling a wagon filled to the top with wires, springs, cardboard, string, fabric, cans, bottles, paper towel tubes, toilet paper rolls . . . (I could go on, but I think I've made my point.) On top of all that stuff is a huge bag of plastic bags.

Lewis glares at them from the front of the line. "I've got loads of stuff at home. I'm bringing it tomorrow."

When Ms. Raffeli walks out to greet us, her face lights up like the 601,736 lights that hold the record for most lights on a residential property (that means a place someone lives in). I have to say, I have never seen Ms. Raffeli this happy. She's definitely happier than when I brought in stuff.

"Oh! What would I do without you two?" she gushes as she leads us to our classroom. "We are definitely winning the inventors' fair this year. I feel it in my bones!"

Ms. Raffeli is so happy she forgets to tell us to hurry and hang up our backpacks, or to get in our groups. Instead, she stands by the wagon, picking through it. She pulls out a piece of fabric and says, "This will be perfect for the baby blanket." She pauses and looks at all the plastic bags. "That's a lot of plastic bags."

Viva shrugs and smiles right at Ms. Raffeli. "You never know when you'll need them."

The rest of us quickly walk away. It's obvious that this is not the time to tell Ms. Raffeli about the world record. The inventors' fair is clearly too important to her. And really, sometimes it's best not to tell grown-ups everything. Their lives are hard enough as it is.

## YOU'D TOTALLY GET IT

Ms. Raffeli says to pull out our sketches and imagine what materials we'll need to make our inventions.

Ny stares at our sketch. "Maybe train tracks," she says, "or Hot Wheels tracks. Something for the plastic bag to attach to and also slide the used bag away from the dog."

"We'll need something to connect everything to the dog," Cornelio says. "Maybe a belt?"

"Great ideas!" Ms. Raffeli leans over. "You've got a winner here."

And maybe it's because she says that, or maybe because we're inventing and breaking a record, but I get that zingy feeling again. "You know what we need?" I say. "A dog!"

Everyone looks at me like I've gone crazy.

Ms. Raffeli's face lights up for a second, then she frowns. "Unfortunately we can't have any dogs in the school unless they are therapy dogs."

"I mean a fake dog," I say. "I don't know how

we make it, but we have to make one so everyone can see how our invention works."

Ms. Raffeli smiles. "I like how you think, Teddy." And she moves on to another group.

Lewis says, "That's what I was going to say."

I don't even get bothered because my brain is too busy trying to think of how to make a fake dog.

## OUR RECORD WILL BE A FIRST

At lunch we all squeeze into the same table. Viva shows us a chart she's making to keep track of how many bags we collect. She tells us about the only two plastic bag records she knows. One is for the most plastic bags collected in eight hours (120,000). She pauses to take a bite of her carrot, then says, "The second one is for a sculpture made out of 68,000 plastic bags. It's in the shape of an octopus!"

Lonnie says, "I'd like to see that in person."

Lewis says, "That's what I was going to say."

Viva sighs and then looks at me. "Teddy, am I forgetting anything?"

"I can't think of any others," I say, peeling a very mushy, very brown banana. I'd rather not eat it, but it's this or the sandwich Dad made on moldy bread. You'd think he'd notice mold!

Lonnie says, "So our record will be a first."

I nod.

Lewis says, "That makes it easy."

"Not necessarily," Lonnie says. "We still need an amazingly large amount of bags, or else the world record people won't take us seriously. Like, more than 120,000 for sure."

Ny's eyes get big. "That's a lot."

Everyone at the table starts talking at once. And even though we are talking about my favorite thing in the world, my banana peel is distracting me. The peel looks like two ears of a dog and the banana looks like a dog's face. Which gets me wondering about how to make a fake dog for our invention.

"Teddy," Lonnie says.

"Sorry," I say, blinking a couple of times.

Lewis says, "You're the one with access to the

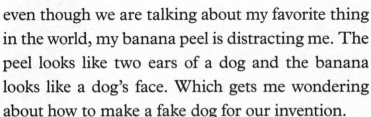

most bags, so we need you to stay focused."

"Right," I say. "Bring in bags. Got it."

While I'm wiping banana off my hand, Lonnie, Viva, and Lewis do a high five; then the lunch monitor rings the bell, and everyone runs through the doors to the playground.

By *everyone* I do mean *everyone*.

Lonnie and Viva don't even wait for me.

That's a first. And even though my feelings are a little hurt, I understand, because I know how exciting breaking a record can be.

It makes your brain do crazy things.

## THAT'S A GOOD QUESTION

At recess, I was hoping we'd all play tag, but the whole group is huddled together looking over the chart, trying to figure out how many bags we need to bring in every day to come close to some kind of record.

Angus is hopping all over the place, which looks like a lot more fun than sitting around doing math. He also looks like a hopping chicken, which makes me laugh.

And thinking about chickens makes me remember the chicken sculptures we made last year in art class out of wire and papier-mâché.

"That's how we can make our dog! Lewis! Cornelio! Ny!" I run over to them, but they don't even look up.

I tap Lewis's shoulder. I think he'd be really excited, since this invention was his idea. "I thought of how to make the dog."

"How can you talk about our invention when we're thinking about our world record?" Lewis asks.

I admit that's a good question, especially for someone like me, who usually only thinks about breaking a record.

And speaking of records, Angus is still hopping. That guy could break a record!

## ALL BY MYSELF

When we go back into our classroom, Lewis, Cornelio, and Ny listen to my idea about the papier-mâché, and they love it. The rest of the day is spent digging through the recycled items, finding things we'll need for our invention. We have plenty of newspapers, which is important for papier-mâché, and even some chicken wire to make the dog shape.

"Am I allowed to bring in flour?" I ask Ms. Raffeli.

"As long as you don't buy it just for this," she says.

We can't believe our luck when we pull out things we can use later, like a belt that will hold our invention onto the dog, and old chair legs that can hold up the track and the plastic bags. Before we know it the bell rings for the end of the day.

For me, this has been the best day ever. I'd stay longer and keep on working, but the rest of my group grabs their stuff while Ms. Raffeli hands out a few pages of reading and heads out the door.

By the time I get outside, no one is around. Max leans out the bus window. "They all took off," he yells, "but Viva said to bring in as many plastic bags tomorrow as you can!"

"Where'd everyone go?" I shout back.

"They all went to Lewis's house," he yells, sticking his head in the window as the bus drives off.

For a few seconds, I stand there in front of school all by myself.

Ms. Raffeli walks out. "Teddy? Is everything all right?"

I nod.

"See you tomorrow," she says, and walks to her car.

Like I said, this has been a really great day, but suddenly the best day ever isn't so great anymore.

## ★ MY TO-DO LIST #11 ★

When I get home, I grab a snack, pull out my to-do list, and add a few things to it.

1. Invent a way to keep The Destructor far from me.
2. Invent a way to keep The Destructor out of the aviary.
3. Break a world record ~~with Lonnie and Viva.~~
4. ~~Get my old desk back.~~

5. ~~Come up with an invention.~~
6. Muddle through school for the rest of the year.
7. Have three seconds alone with Lonnie and Viva.
8. Survive breaking a record with a lot of people.
9. Bring in plastic bags.
10. Bring in more wire.
11. Bring in flour.

## ONE GOOD THING

After dinner I grab as many plastic bags from Caitlin and Casey as I can while they fight over plastic bottles. I can't believe my luck when I find more chicken wire.

I don't ask if I can have it; I just take it.

I'm stuffing all the plastic bags into one large trash bag when Mom says to Dad, "Please try and get Jake out of the pigeon costume. We need to wash it."

"Where are you going?" Dad asks.

"I'm doing the trash."

"But I cooked," Dad says. As if that means

something, considering dinner was chicken so burnt that you needed a saw to cut through it, and broccoli that was so overcooked it melted in your mouth.

Instead of answering him, Mom lugs the bag outside.

Dad looks at The Destructor. The Destructor looks at Dad.

Dad says, "This is not a problem."

"Coo! Coo!" The Destructor does not sound happy.

"We can do this. Right, Jake?" But instead of answering Dad, The Destructor squawks out of the room.

"How does your mother do this?" Dad mutters, and runs after him.

I reach into the cabinet and grab the bag of flour. In some families, you need to ask before taking a bag of flour. I guess that's the one good thing about mine, no one notices anything!

## INVENTORS VS. THE DESTRUCTOR

The next morning as I walk into the aviary to feed the birds, I get slammed in the face with something.

167

"Ow!" I scream, and pull off another wad of wet paper.

"Oh." The Destructor shrugs. "It's you. I thought you'd never wake up. Not even the alarm on my watch woke you up, and it beeps really loud."

I glare at him. "What is with you and that slingshot?"

"Just doing my job."

"And what exactly is your job?"

"I'm Pigeon Boy, protector of the pigeons!" He jumps onto a bucket, sticks out his chest, and holds his slingshot high. "Coo! Coo!"

"Well, I'm not here to hurt them," I say. "I'm here to feed them."

"If you're going to feed the pigeons," The Destructor says, still standing on the bucket, "you've got to get up early in the morning."

"I do get here early," I say.

"But not as early as me," he says. "And that's why I fed them."

"You fed them?" I say.

"Yeah, they seemed hungry."

"That's because it's the morning!" I say. "And I feed them in the morning. *Me!* Not you!"

"Admiral Ackbar was getting grumpy."

"He's always grumpy!" I yell.

"Don't shout," The Destructor whispers. "It scares the birds."

"Argh!" I say, and storm out.

One of the things I learned from my homework is that inventors were not always nice to each other. It's awful to think about, but sometimes they stole ideas from one another. I guess some people call this being dedicated; I call it lousy.

And stealing is exactly what The Destructor is doing to me. He's stealing my aviary, my Grumpy Pigeon Man, my job! And he doesn't see anything wrong with it. Well, I've had enough. The only way to fight him is to be like him, which means acting like a miserable, thieving inventor.

I do not think this will be easy, but it will be necessary.

## THE BEST WAY TO ORGANIZE

Mom couldn't drive me to school this morning even though I had a full trash bag of plastic bags to carry. Mom couldn't drive me because she has to work on the plumbing in the downstairs bathroom. She has to work on the plumbing because it turns out that for days The Destructor has been stuffing pigeon feathers down the toilet. He did this because he wanted to clean the aviary and the toilet was the best place to dump the evidence. Since the evidence was mostly poo.

Nothing happened until this morning, when I used the toilet and it overflowed. Feathers went all over the floor and all over me!

Anyway, the plastic bags aren't all that heavy, but they did slow me down a little. I was also slowed down because I needed to find dry sneakers, so I was late to school.

When I walk into class, Lonnie and Viva rush over to help.

"Look at all of them," Lonnie says.

Viva sits down on the bag like it's a chair.

"Did you get new sneakers?" Lonnie asks.

"You don't want to know."

This is not true, of course he wants to know, but luckily Ms. Raffeli walks over right then. "That's a lot of plastic bags."

"You never know when someone will need a plastic bag," I say.

"Good thinking," she says, and wanders away to help Team #1 with a wheel issue.

Ny walks over with a clipboard. "How many bags did you bring in?" She sees I'm confused. "It's for this chart."

"I thought Viva made a chart?"

"Our charts are different. Hers was for how many we need to collect. Mine is for how many bags we *have* collected."

Lewis steps in between us. "So far we have thirty."

Viva pushes Lewis out of the way. "But that doesn't include the bags Lonnie and I brought yesterday. We have to count those up today at recess."

Lewis holds a rolled-up ball of plastic bags about the same size as a tennis ball.

Lonnie says, "We tied the ends of the bags together and then rolled them up."

"It's the best way to organize them," Viva says.

"When did you do that?" I ask.

"This morning," Lewis says, tossing it up and down. "We got here early. If you're going to break a world record, you've got to get up early."

I think about this. I know it's true because The Destructor gets up early, and he's about to break a world record for most annoying brother in the world.

## THE DOG

I pull out the wire and the flour I took from our kitchen and we all get to work. Ny and I bend the chicken wire into the shape of a tall dog. Lewis directs us, and I don't even mind because I'm having so much fun. "Longer legs," he says. "Bigger ears, or he'll look like a tall cat," he says. "Don't forget the tail. My dog has a tail."

By lunchtime, we've got the dog halfway covered in papier-mâché.

Ms. Raffeli comes over. "Oh!" she says. "It's wonderful." Her eyes actually fill up with tears and she hugs me. "Good thinking, Teddy."

It's nice to feel like I'm getting something right.

## TOP OF THE WORLD

"We've got to get the word out that we need plastic bags," Lonnie says, taking a bite out of a sandwich that looks really good.

"We need to make posters," Viva says as she takes a bite of her yogurt. Yogurt is not my favorite, but it's still better than the dry crackers I have in my lunch today.

"That's what I was going to say," Lewis says.

Viva shakes her head. "And because we need to make posters, I've brought markers and paper."

Lewis doesn't say anything.

During recess, some of us sit around tying plastic bags to each other and adding them to the plastic bag ball we already have, while Cornelio checks off how many bags we have. And some of us make posters.

By the end of recess, we have a plastic bag ball as big as a beach ball, we have three posters asking for plastic bag donations, and we have a bunch of kids feeling like they're on top of the world.

### GRACE NEEDS NEWS

I'm in the kitchen inventing possible ways to keep The Destructor out of the aviary.

1. Superglue him to his bed.
2. Set up a giant net that drops on him when he opens Grumpy Pigeon Man's gate.
3. Throw bars of chocolate at him every morning and afternoon. He forgets about everything when there's chocolate around.

I'm trying to come up with number four when Grace walks in.

"Pay attention," she says. "Pay very close attention. I need a good story for the newspaper."

"Are you asking for advice from me?"

"No way."

"Then what?"

"I'm punishing you for ruining my career. The only story they want now is about kids doing wacky things. I'm a serious reporter. This was not supposed to happen."

Mom walks in with a bag of groceries just as Grace slams on my foot.

"Ow!" I howl.

"Teddy," Mom says. "Quiet down. Jake is napping under the table. I don't know why he's so tired lately."

"Maybe he wakes up too early," I suggest.

"I'm not tired!" The Destructor hollers from under the table. "And I wasn't napping!"

I hop out of the room and take my list with me. Mom just gave me another idea.

4. Keep him awake all night so that he sleeps all day.

## FRIED EGG

Later that afternoon, I look at the clock on the kitchen wall and head out to the aviary to feed the pigeons. I know The Destructor will be there, because he wasn't in the house. What I didn't know is that he'd be pretending to fly around. "Coo! Coo!" When he sees me, he stops and says, "We're letting them out."

Some people might not know what this means, but I do. The pigeons are going to fly free. Grumpy Pigeon Man hasn't let them out for months.

"I was going to feed them," I say.

"You feed them after they fly, not before," Grumpy Pigeon Man says. "Or else they won't come home."

Grumpy Pigeon Man opens the door and shoos the pigeons through it. The Destructor runs around helping him.

At first they don't know what to do and flutter down on the roof, until Admiral Ackbar takes to the sky, and then they all follow. They fly up, staying together and flapping around in a circle.

"You haven't let them out in a long time," I say.

"Have to wait for the leaves to come out on the trees."

"Why's that?"

"Protection."

Sometimes I wonder if he talks like this just to make me ask questions. "From what?" I ask.

"From hawks, of course," The Destructor interrupts. "Hawks are the enemy to pigeons." Grumpy Pigeon Man must have already told him all about this. It's the only way he'd know.

"When I was a sailor, it was seagulls we had to worry about." Grumpy Pigeon Man stares into the sky. "Here it's the hawks."

The Destructor holds up his slingshot.

"What are you doing with that?" I ask.

"Remember?" he says. "Protector of pigeons?"

I leave those two and go to my backyard. I lie down in the grass to watch the pigeons flying.

Suddenly, something hits me. I'm pretty sure it's bird poo, because it has happened before. I stand up and look, but it's not bird poo, it's a fried egg! A very cold fried egg.

"Can I have my egg back?" The Destructor yells through the fence.

"You hit me with a fried egg?"

"I wasn't aiming at you. I thought I saw a hawk."

"So how come I got hit?"

"I can't control where they land."

He climbs over the fence. "I really need my egg back," he says, snatching for it. He grabs his egg and, as he

climbs back over to Grumpy Pigeon Man's yard, shouts, "At least it isn't runny!"

That might be the one thing The Destructor and I have ever agreed on.

## THAT NIGHT

While The Destructor is asleep, I sneak over to him and pick up his wrist. Nothing wakes him. I take off his watch, turn off the alarm, and stick it in my sock drawer. This was not on my list of possible ways to keep The Destructor out of the aviary, because I just thought of it as I was going to bed. And even though I like the superglue idea more, this is much easier. Without his watch, he won't wake up, and the aviary will be mine once more.

My job is done.

## THAT MORNING

I wake up. I look over at The Destructor's bed. He's still fast asleep. I sneak out of the room and go to the bathroom. I've left all my clothes there so I won't wake him while I get dressed. Of course I forgot to get socks, so I duck back into our room

179

and open my sock drawer. I'm just about to close it when a beep, beep, beeping starts up. I freeze, but the beeping keeps going. That's when I start looking for the watch. I know I turned the alarm off, so why is it beeping? I dig through my socks.

I pull it out right when he asks, "How'd my watch get in there?"

"Weird," I say, handing him the watch. "Very weird." I head out of the room, followed by The Destructor's footsteps.

## A WHOLE WEEK

Strange but true, the fastest thing in the universe is the speed of light. But scientists have discovered these particles called neutrinos that I guess are maybe even faster. For me, however, the fastest thing in the world is school because I've never had so much fun!

We've been working nonstop on our inventions. The dog looks great. Ny painted it black and brown, and Cornelio drew really cute eyes and a nose. And we all worked on the part that collects the poo. It's incredible!

We made a frame that goes on the dog. We attached the train track to the frame with wire.

Then we attached a bag to a clothes hanger that we hooked onto the track. The bag hangs down under the dog. When there is something heavy in the bag, like poo, the train track bends, and that makes the hanger slide along the track and away from the dog, so the person walking the dog can tie up the bag and throw it away. It's really great.

The other inventions are pretty good, too.

Lonnie, Viva, Serena, and Max's battery-operated trash compactor works really good on soft, mushy things. They know this because they put an old plastic bucket in it, and the compactor, which is actually a box, broke. Luckily for them, their invention still works, but now it's covered in duct tape. It was a good thing Viva's family had a lot of duct tape!

The Go Kid Go Wagon is also pretty cool. It's like a giant windup toy. It can fit three kids, but Ms. Raffeli won't let us try it out in the hall because she's so worried about spies.

The musical blanket has really taken off. It turns out we all want to snuggle with something that is soft, cozy, and plays music.

After doing all this work on our invention, I understand Ms. Raffeli a lot better. And now even without a prize, I really want to win. I think that's true for the whole class.

But I have to say, I'm not worried. I feel it in my bones. Our invention is sure to win.

## MORE PLASTIC BAGS?

Besides the inventions going so well, our plastic bag ball keeps growing. It's as tall as five desks, as wide as the bookcase, and lives in the classroom library.

After the other kids in the class heard about what we were doing, they started bringing in bags, too. We had to swear them to secrecy, which wasn't a problem since we all understand that grown-ups don't always appreciate the same things kids do—like breaking world records for example. Occasionally, Ms. Raffeli asks if we have enough bags now. We nod, but then we bring more in anyway. So far, this strategy is working for us.

Thanks to Caitlin and Casey, I always bring in a lot of bags. But also, Lonnie and Viva made a bunch more posters asking for plastic bags for their trash masher. They stuck them all over school.

After they put up the posters, we got so many donations that we had to set up a bin in the front hall so people had a place to leave their bags. I have a feeling most of the kids in the school know we're trying to break a record, but somehow they also know not to say a word to any teachers.

Sometimes Ms. Raffeli notices all the bags. But she's got so much on her mind that she doesn't think about it for too long.

At least, that's what I think.

## THE BATHROOM

Mom has decided to totally redo the downstairs bathroom.

By redo I do mean destroy.

"Easter is this weekend," she says. "And Gran is coming. I want this bathroom to be in working order. I'm putting in a new sink, and of course a new toilet."

I'm glad she's replacing the toilet, but it means we only have one bathroom to use as a bathroom.

Mom must know what I'm thinking, because she says, "Don't worry. I'll be done in two days. Three days at the most."

I hope she's right. Boy, do I hope she's right.

## ★ MY TO-DO LIST #12 ★

Now that Mom reminded me about Easter, I can't stop thinking about dyeing eggs. I love dyeing eggs. Mom always bought loads of eggs, but now that she's making Dad do the grocery shopping, I'm worried he'll forget to buy them. He forgets to buy a lot of stuff, like my favorite cereal, for instance. And even though weeks ago we had cartons of eggs, now with Dad in charge, we don't have any.

I pull out my list. It's looking pretty shabby,

torn, and hard to read. I think it went through the laundry. So, I throw it away and start a brand-new one. A list with a lot less words so I won't get distracted or forget a thing. I think I'm finally getting the hang of the to-do list.

1. Buy eggs
2. Dye eggs
3. Plastic bags
4. Inventors' fair
5. The Destructor

## LARGEST EXPLOSIONS IN THE SOLAR SYSTEM

We're coloring in the poster about our invention when I realize that as great as our invention is, something is missing. "We've been thinking so much about the invention," I say, "but not the presentation. People need something to look at. Something to remember."

"How do we do that?" Ny asks.

Then I gasp. I bounce up and down. "Why didn't we think of this before? The blanket makes music. The trash compactor compacts. The Go Kid Go Wagon goes. Our dog needs to poo!"

"Poo?" Cornelio says.

"Poo?" Ny says.

"I was *not* going to say that," Lewis says.

"Not real poo. Fake poo," I say.

Ms. Raffeli comes over right then. "Did someone say poo?" There is something very weird about your teacher using the word poo, but I get over it quick because I'm so excited about my idea.

"I did!" I say. "We don't just invent poo, but even better, we invent a way for the poo to actually come out of the dog, so everyone sees the invention in action!"

Lewis, Ny, and Cornelio look at me like I just broke the record for fastest woman to run the 100-meter hurdles in swim flippers (18.523 seconds). Yes, running and jumping in swim flippers!

There are a few moments of silence, and then Ms. Raffeli says, "I love it! I absolutely love it." She wipes her eyes. I think I made her cry from happiness.

As incredible as massive explosions on the sun must be, making your teacher cry from joy—twice in one year—is even more incredible!

## PULLING OUT NAILS

At lunch, things are a little strange. Lonnie and Viva sit across from Lewis and don't talk.

"What's going on?" I ask.

Viva rolls her eyes. "Two weeks to go and someone thinks we aren't doing enough to break the record." She jerks her eyeballs across to Lewis.

Lewis glares at her. "*You* said *I* wasn't doing enough."

"She didn't say that," Lonnie says. "She said Teddy was bringing in the most bags."

"I've been counting all those bags," Lewis says.

Viva sighs. "I know you have."

Lewis puts his sandwich down. "You couldn't break this record without me."

Now Lonnie puts his sandwich down. "That seems like an exaggeration."

Ny scoots closer. "Lewis has done a lot."

"What about you two?" Cornelio says.

"We made more posters." Lonnie sits up straighter.

Serena says, "That was weeks ago."

"It was one week ago," Viva says. "And I thought you were on our team."

"I might be working on an invention with you, but these guys are my friends, too." She flips her hair and, of course, hits Viva in the face.

So Viva flips her hair, only because it's short, it doesn't hit Serena's face.

Then Lewis crosses his arms. "I don't even know why I agreed to do this with you."

And that's when Lonnie's and Viva's mouths drop open like they're about to break the record for most grapes caught in the mouth in three minutes (233).

But then they shut them and Viva crosses her arms. "Fine. We do it on our own."

Lewis stands up. "Fine. Who's on my team?" Ny, Cornelio, and Serena raise their hands.

Then Lonnie stands up. "Who's with us?" Max and Angus raise their hands.

Viva looks at me. "What about Teddy?"

"There's only

one thing to do," Lonnie says, as if he's already a Jedi. "We share him. Any bags Teddy brings in are split between us."

"You're joking," I say.

Viva says, "Why would you think we're joking?"

"That's what I was going to say." Lewis glares at her.

Strange but true, the record for the fastest time to pull 5 nails out of a piece of wood with your teeth is 7.44 seconds. I never thought anyone could pull nails with their teeth, but then again, I never thought our class record would suddenly turn into a competition, and it just did.

## EDISON'S WORDS

Pulling out nails with your teeth cannot be comfortable. I can say the same for recess today. I hope the afternoon is better. But as we walk back into the classroom, I can tell it won't be, because as Lewis hangs up his coat, he says, "We'll have to stay this afternoon and divide the bags."

"Fine," Viva says.

"No problem." Lonnie shrugs.

"I'll call my mom," Ny says.

Cornelio nods. "Me too."

"Can anyone think of a way to make fake poo?" I ask. "Pinecones? Sausages? Tootsie Rolls?"

No one says a word. I think about Edison and what he said about finding ten thousand ways to fail. So I keep talking since I'm not even close to ten thousand, and it's more fun to think about this than about my friends fighting. "Mud? No, too runny." And then it comes to me. "Chocolate pudding! Frozen chocolate pudding in the shape of poo."

Lonnie, Viva, and Lewis shake their heads at me and go to their desks, which is how I learn that a classroom can be more uncomfortable than pulling nails out of wood with my teeth. Luckily,

the thought of making chocolate pudding poo
makes everything a lot easier.

## NO ONE EVEN ASKS ME

Finally it's the end of the day. Lonnie, Viva, Max,
and Angus are standing in one clump. Lewis,
Ny, Cornelio, and Serena are huddled in another
clump. Ms. Raffeli is in the middle.

"So let me get this straight," Ms. Raffeli says.
"Now you're going to divide the bags into two
piles? I don't understand any of it, but if you feel
like you need to, go ahead. I've got some copying
to do." She walks out. The two groups get to work
on the bags.

It's weird, but even though there are a million
things at home that make me miserable, staying
here has to be worse, so I slip away, and to be honest, no one even asks me to stay.

## POO

That night I toss and turn. I can't fall asleep. My
brain is too mixed up. So I eventually go downstairs to scrounge around for a snack. I'm looking

behind all the normal stuff, because we all know Dad hides his favorite snacks, hoping none of us will find them. That's when I see the instant chocolate pudding! I can't believe my luck. It's exactly what I need. I knew Dad loved chocolate pudding, but I didn't know we had any.

And since I'm awake anyway, I decide to make it. It's easy, just add water and stir. After it's all mixed, I scoop small blobs onto plastic wrap, roll them up in a sausage shape, and stick them in the freezer. They really look like poo!

Now I've just got to think of how to push them out of the dog.

It's amazing how much happiness I get from working on my invention. I thought I could only be this happy breaking records. It turns out I was wrong!

## SO TIRED

This morning I finally wake up from the beeping noise of a watch. The Destructor is pulling on his pigeon costume. And even though I'm so tired I could use my head holder invention, when The Destructor says, "Don't worry. I'll feed the pigeons," I leap out of bed.

"Think again, Destructor!"

"Pigeon Boy!" he screams, and chases me down the stairs. I run to the sink, where I left the dirty chocolate pudding bowl and spoon.

I grab them and wave them in front of The Destructor's face. "Look, pudding!" The Destructor cannot resist chocolate. He sticks his head right in the bowl as I race out to the aviary.

And just as I hoped, I finish all my jobs and he still hasn't shown up.

One win for me.

As satisfying as this is, I know it can't last—unless, of course, I figure out how to make chocolate pudding every day. And that's about as likely as me breaking the record for most iron bars bent in one minute (26). So I'm definitely going to have to think of another way to keep him out of the aviary!

## NO ONE NEEDS TO KNOW

The Destructor is under the table grumbling about how I tricked him, while I take out the little frozen poos. Dad walks in as I drop them into a bag with an ice pack to keep them cold.

"Is that poo?" he asks.

"It's for my invention," I say. He has no idea how happy he just made me.

"I don't even want to know," he says.

"It's delicious!" The Destructor says from under the table.

Dad shakes his head. "Like I said, I don't want to know." He walks out of the room.

I pick up my backpack, and even though the world record doesn't seem as fun, I did promise my friends I'd bring more bags, so I stop at the front door, grab the big bag of plastic bags that Caitlin and Casey gave to me.

By the time I get to the blacktop, I'm dragging the bag. Lonnie and Viva see me and rush over to help me.

"This is awesome," Viva says as we make our way into the line. I look around, but no one else from our class is in line, not even Lewis.

"Yesterday, Viva and I went around my neighborhood," Lonnie says. "We collected a lot of bags." He points to the bag next to him. It's not very big.

"I think Lewis planned this the whole time," Viva says.

Lonnie nods. "I wouldn't be surprised if he shows up with a huge amount of plastic bags."

Viva says, "He kept saying he was going to bring some in but never did."

"And now when he does bring them," Lonnie says, "he won't have to share."

"That seems complicated," I say.

"Lewis is a complicated kid," Lonnie says.

Viva crosses her arms. "You know he'll stop at nothing to win."

"That's why we thought you could give us all your bags," Lonnie says.

"What?"

"Just this one time," Lonnie says. "To even things out."

"No one will ever know," Viva says.

Strange but true, the record for most concrete blocks broken on a stomach in one minute is 8. Right now, I feel like someone just broke a million blocks on my stomach.

## THE BIG BANG

Right then Lewis shows up, followed by Ny, Cornelio, and Serena. And just like Lonnie and Viva said, Lewis is dragging a huge bag behind him. It's actually bigger than mine.

"See!" Viva says. "He wanted this to be a competition the whole time."

Lonnie says, "It sure looks like he was holding out on us."

"Just pretend your bag is ours," Viva says. "And ours is yours."

"It's the only way to make this fair," Lonnie says and dumps my bag down next to him in line.

"We did pretty well last night, don't you think?" Viva says this extra loud. Clearly she wants Lewis to hear every word. Then she leans over and whispers, "No one will know."

Lewis looks at the bag that he *thinks* is mine, but is *actually* Lonnie and Viva's. "Is that all you brought, Teddy?"

I can't say anything. I just look away.

"Oh brother!" Viva says. "What about all your bags, Lewis? I thought you didn't have any."

The big bang holds the world record for greatest explosion ever. Considering it created everything in our universe and everything beyond our universe, it definitely deserves the record. But right after Viva says that stuff about Lewis's bags, the second largest explosion takes place. And I think I understand this explosion better than the big bang, because this explosion involved a lot kids yelling at each other about plastic bags.

I have to say, I wish Ms. Raffeli would come out soon, because competition really does not bring out the best in these people.


## FROZEN POO

It's all thanks to Ms. Raffeli and her eyebrows that my class finally lines up and makes it to the classroom silently. Those eyebrows have a lot of power when they are raised as tall as the tallest building in the world (Burj Khalifa).

Our classroom looks so different now that there are two plastic bag balls instead of one. The balls look smaller and sadder and more lonely. One is close to Lonnie and Viva's group and the other is close to our group. Serena does not seem happy sitting with Lonnie and Viva anymore. I can tell by the number of times she whacks Viva in the face with her hair.

I pull out the little frozen poos from their bag

and show them to my team. "What do you think? They look really good, right?" But no one is looking at the chocolate pudding poo I made.

They're all staring behind me.

And then I look at what they're all staring at: the plastic bags.

"Sorry," Ny says. "Did you say something?"

I admit, I am surprised that plastic bags get more attention than my fake poo.

As my gran likes to say, "What's the world coming to?"

## 233 OYSTERS

Sitting somewhere else at lunch has never been an option for me. In fact, I've always thought that it would be worse than eating 233 oysters in three minutes.

But today, for the first time in my life, I can tell from across the lunchroom that I'd rather break the oyster record than sit at my usual table. Lonnie, Viva, Angus, and Max are on one side of the table and Lewis, Ny, Cornelio,

and Serena are on the other side. There is no talking, just a lot of glaring.

Before any of my friends see me, I sneak quietly backward and find a different table far away.

It clearly doesn't matter, because no one even notices.

## A BIG MESS

Jasmine B. and Jasmine H. are sitting at a table across the room. This seems a much better choice.

Jasmine B. and Jasmine H. don't look surprised when I sit down.

"I knew this would happen," Jasmine B. says.

Jasmine H. nods her head. "It was only a matter of time."

I don't know what to say, so I look through my lunch for something to eat. Dad made a mushed banana sandwich. Really, what does he think I am, a baby? I guess I shouldn't complain; at least the bread isn't moldy today.

"Things like this always happen," Jasmine B. says. She has soup today. It smells really good.

"What do you mean?" I ask.

Jasmine H. dips her cucumber into hummus. I like cucumber and hummus. "When people try and do something together, it always ends in disaster. Don't you watch reality TV?"

I shake my head. "I don't get much TV time with my family."

Jasmine B. takes out a cupcake. I'm so hungry I actually think I should eat the frozen chocolate pudding poo that I brought in, but even though I know it's fake, it still seems gross.

I must look hungry, because Jasmine B. says, "It was my sister's birthday yesterday." She stuffs the whole cupcake in her mouth. "If I were you, I'd get out of this record-breaking thing."

Jasmine H. nods. "If it's anything like *Family Bake-Off*, you're in trouble."

Jasmine B. licks her fingers. "So true. So true."

"What happens in *Family Bake-Off*?"

And just like how my sisters Caitlin and Casey say things at the same time, Jasmine B. and Jasmine H. look at each other and say, "It all ends in a big mess."

I'm thinking about what kind of mess this could end in when the bell rings for recess.

I stand up and Jasmine B. says, "Whatever you do, don't let them find you at recess."

"Why not?"

Jasmine H. says, "Don't say we didn't warn you."

## A BIG MESS PART 2

I should have listened to the two Jasmines, but it's not easy to hide from friends.

Strange but true, the world record for largest tug-of-war in the world was broken by 1,574 people. That must have been pretty stressful. There was probably a lot of screaming and shouting. And it had to be especially hard on the rope. All those people, pulling it in two opposite directions.

Recess feels exactly like tug-of-war, and I feel exactly like the rope.

And it's my own fault. The two Jasmines
warned me.

## SHE BELIEVES IN ME

At the end of the school day, Ms. Raffeli makes
an announcement. "Clearly, we've all been a little
too caught up in inventions to remember the holi-
days. But thanks to the two Jasmines, I've been
reminded that there is a long weekend."

Ms. Raffeli sighs deeply and then continues. "As much as I hate to miss a single day of
school during such an important project, we will.
Tomorrow, Friday, we don't have school."

There is a collective whoop from everyone.
Ms. Raffeli looks surprised by this, like she can't
imagine wanting to be anywhere but here. "Some
of you celebrate Passover, some celebrate Easter,
and some celebrate a day off of school."

"I do all three," Viva says. Because her mom
is Jewish and her dad is Christian, Viva celebrates
everything.

Ms. Raffeli continues talking. "Whatever you
do, please keep in mind that the inventors' fair is
only a week away. If we want to win we need to
use all the time we've got left. So over the days off,

think about your invention. What can you add? What can you change? How can you make it better? Remember, inventors never stop thinking!"

I really agree with Ms. Raffeli, but what are the chances I can figure out how to push poo out of our invention over Easter weekend? I mean, Gran will be visiting, Mom hasn't finished the bathroom, and I even forgot to remind Dad to buy eggs! (Which is really infuriating because what's the point of having a list if I forget to look at it?)

Then Ms. Raffeli says, "The last and most important thing I want you to know is that no matter what is going on over the weekend, I believe in you." And she looks straight at me when she says this.

And suddenly I believe in myself. Nothing will stop me. Not The Destructor, not Easter, not broken toilets or crazy sisters or forgetful fathers, not even breaking a world record.

If Ms. Raffeli believes I can do it, then so do I.

## THE MOST POWERFUL POWER

When I walk outside, I find I've walked into the middle of another tug-of-war about those dumb plastic bags.

"There's no way you can beat us!" Viva says.

Lewis says, "We have a power you don't even know about!"

"The only power I'm feeling from you is the power of the dark side," Lonnie says.

Ny says, "I know all about your power and our power will destroy your power."

"Your power doesn't come close to our power." Angus bounces at her feet.

Max says, "That's not possible, because our power is the most powerful."

Serena says, "How can you say your power is the most powerful when our power is?"

"Because he just did," Viva says, and her eyes get all big. "We said it first, so it's ours."

I never thought I'd say this, but I'm tired of record breaking.

## GRAN'S ADVICE

Gran is in the kitchen reading the paper when I get home. There are a bunch of presents on the table. Gran always brings presents. The Destructor has already opened his. It's a play-dough pasta-making kit. I pick up the box and look at the pictures. The kit can make over five different kinds of pasta, just from squishing the play dough through the different tubes. Gran gives me a book. She always gives me books. This one is called *Inventions*.

I give her a hug. "Where's Mom?"

"Working on that toilet of hers."

"I wonder if she'll ever finish," I say.

"I heard that!" Mom shouts. "I'm almost done."

"Sure," Gran says. She winks at me and whispers, "Your mom has always been an optimist."

I don't normally ask my gran personal questions, but today I feel like I need some advice. "Hey, Gran? Have you ever had a hard time with friends?"

"Who hasn't?" she says. "My best friend Tina Capriano is a pain beyond all pains! Once she stole my blueberry pie recipe, made it, and won first prize at the county fair."

"But you're still friends?"

"Of course. Why wouldn't we be? I just keep my recipes locked up."

I think about this and wonder what I would lock up. Besides The Destructor, of course.

## SO MAD

When I walk over to feed the birds, I see them flying outside again. And Grumpy Pigeon Man and The Destructor are standing outside watching them. The Destructor has his slingshot raised and ready to shoot if any hawk comes too close.

"Don't take your eyes off them," Grumpy Pigeon Man says.

The Destructor holds his arms steady. "I won't."

"A hawk can appear out of nowhere."

The Destructor says, "I'll be ready."

"I know you will." Grumpy Pigeon Man pats him on the back. "It takes dedication to care for pigeons. You can't be doing nine million other things. Pigeons need our full attention." And even though he's talking to The Destructor, I know he's actually talking to me. And it makes me so mad I feel like I could break the record for crushing the most watermelons with my head in one minute (43).

I think about Gran's advice, and suddenly I know what I need to lock up. Me. I'm locking myself up. Grumpy Pigeon Man doesn't deserve to have me!

I march up to Grumpy Pigeon Man. "I quit," I say. "And don't try to change my mind."

As I stomp back to my house, I wait for him to shout after me. But he doesn't.

Of course he doesn't.

## HIDING THE BAGS

After I walk away from The Destructor and Grumpy Pigeon Man, I actually feel strangely free.

And that feeling helps me figure out what I'm going to do about the plastic bag record, too.

When Caitlin and Casey come home and finish weighing their trash, they hand over all the plastic bags they found. Normally, I leave them by the door so I don't forget to bring them to school.

Today I sneak them upstairs to my room. I open my closet and shove them all the way into the back. There's no way anyone will find them there.

I'm locking them up for good!

### ★ MY TO-DO LIST #13 ★

1. Buy eggs (Remind Dad to buy eggs!!!)
2. Dye eggs
3. ~~Plastic bags~~
4. Inventors' fair

5. ~~The Destructor~~

6. Find something to push out the poo.


## FRIDAY

It's Friday, and a day off from school.

Usually this makes no difference to me, because I always wake up early to feed the pigeons. But today I don't. Today I pretend to be asleep while The Destructor puts on his pigeon costume and goes out. Today I try and stay in bed, but I can't.

I get up and stare out the window. From my window, I have a perfect view of Grumpy Pigeon Man's yard. I watch Grumpy Pigeon Man shuffle out to the aviary. I go back to bed. I just wanted to be sure the birds were okay.

The bad thing about staying in bed is how boring it is. Even reading *The Guinness Book of World Records* doesn't make me feel better.

But I'm not moving. I don't care how bad I feel. I'm staying right here. And then Gran calls, "Pancakes!" And I hop out of bed faster than a cheetah, the fastest land mammal, because if there were a world record for most delicious pancakes, Gran would break it.

## TOP SECRET

After breakfast, Caitlin and Casey have more bags for me. I'm sneaking them into my room when Gran comes out of the bathroom.

"What have you got there, Teddy?"

"Nothing," I say, hiding the bags behind me and backing away.

I close my bedroom door and smoosh the bags into the back of my closet. To be extra careful, I pile clothes on top of the bags so it looks like a pile of clothes.

And even though I'm following Gran's advice, which should mean it's okay, I've got a feeling this needs to be top secret. And that means from everybody.

Even Gran.

## SATURDAY

Since I don't have my job at the aviary anymore, I spend Saturday morning sitting around in the kitchen with Gran reading about inventions from the book she gave me.

There's a knock on our front door. Because Mom is working in the bathroom, Gran answers it. "Teddy?" she calls. "Someone named Stewis is here to see you."

"Lewis," he says.

"Sorry," Gran says.

My first impulse is to look for somewhere to hide, but before I can, Gran walks into the kitchen. "What are you waiting for?" she asks. "An invitation from the queen?"

I go outside. Lewis, Ny, Cornelio, and Serena are crowded on the front steps.

Lewis says, "We thought we'd make your life easier and pick up any bags you have."

Ny says, "We'll count them and give half to Lonnie and Viva."

I know I decided not to give them any more bags, but I hadn't thought about lying to their faces. I wonder if I should just go upstairs and get the bags out of the closet. But right then Lonnie walks up, followed by Viva, Angus, and Max.

"Oh brother!" Viva says. "We should have known you'd be sneaking around!"

"I could say the same thing about you," Lewis says.

Ny says, "We came to pick up bags."

Angus says, "So did we."

"But we were going to share them," Ny says.

"So were we!" I've never heard Angus sound

mad, but he just did.

And just like that, my mind clears and I know what I'm going to do. "I'm sorry," I lie. "Caitlin and Casey recycled all the bags before I could stop them."

Every face drops. That's when Gran walks out. "Well, aren't you going to introduce me to your friends?" The Destructor peeks out from behind her legs.

Lonnie waves to Gran. "Hi, Teddy's gran!" He's the only one who has met Gran before.

"Lonnie!" she says. "Your family's coming over tomorrow for Easter. And where's that Viva girl?"

Viva raises her hand.

"Your family, too." Gran smiles and stands there staring at everyone.

Then Lewis grumbles, "We've got work to do."

Viva says, "Us too."

And like the record for most people to vanish in a magic trick (100), my friends disappear.

## IT'S HARD TO DYE EGGS WHEN . . .

1. Mom dashes out to the hardware store because she needs a part for the toilet.
2. The only eggs we have are brown. I should

be happy Dad remembered them at all.

3. Gran takes a nap.

4. Sharon leaves because, in her words, "I have a stupid rehearsal!"

5. Caitlin and Casey would rather fight over who collected the most trash today.

6. Maggie dyes four eggs, then says, "If I'm ever going to beat Bella Colon, I can't sit here dyeing eggs all day," and goes for her run.

7. Grace says, "Dyeing eggs is for babies." Then she stomps on my foot.

8. The Destructor shows up, plunks any egg he can grab into every color we have, so they all come out even browner than they started, and then runs back to the aviary.

9. Dad comes home and asks me why the kitchen is a mess.

## EASTER SUNDAY SURPRISE

It's a holiday, but I still wake up early. I wonder how long it'll take until I can sleep longer. I was already awake when The Destructor left. I lie in bed for a little, and then I sit up. It's Easter! That means Easter baskets! Next to Halloween, Easter is the best candy holiday. I run downstairs.

Strange but true, the fish with the most eyes is the six-eyed spookfish. I do not need six eyes to know that The Destructor is already in the kitchen. The sound of crinkling wrappers says it all. This is definitely not the surprise I wanted.

The Destructor lies in the middle of the floor surrounded by candy wrappers. Chocolate is smeared all over his face, and next to him there are two baskets—TWO EMPTY EASTER BASKETS.

The Destructor doesn't move or say hello. Clearly he's in some kind of candy haze.

I look on the table and I count five baskets.

They are lined up in a perfect row. Each basket has a name on it. I read them: *Sharon, Caitlin, Casey, Maggie,* and *Grace.*

I don't need to, but I crouch down and read the tags of the baskets on the floor: *Jake* and *Teddy.*

Suddenly, The Destructor sits up, lets out a moan, and then pukes all over me.

Next year, I'm writing to the Easter Bunny, telling him not to leave a basket for my brother. He doesn't deserve it.

## GOOD-LUCK EGG

If I'd known the vomit smell would stick to me like the record for most sticky notes stuck to a person in five minutes (674), I would have destroyed The Destructor. But I can't because the doorbell rings and Lonnie's and Viva's families arrive at the same time.

Viva's dad says, "Thanks for inviting us."

"What's that smell?" Viva's mom asks.

Luckily Mom says, "Just so you know, the downstairs toilet is not working," and leads everyone into the living room.

The Destructor is still out with Grumpy Pigeon Man. Sharon is ignoring Jerome, Caitlin and Casey are ignoring each other, Maggie is talking about running with Gran, who used to be a track star, and Grace is eavesdropping. Or as she tells me it's called in the newspaper business, "Looking for a good story."

"Can we hide eggs?" Lonnie asks.

"Oh, I love hiding eggs," Viva says.

Lonnie and Viva are acting like the whole plastic bag thing never happened, so I do too. I grab the two dozen eggs that we dyed earlier, and we head upstairs. The way the game works is that two of us hide the eggs, and the third person looks. Then we switch.

Lonnie and I are hiding eggs for Viva when Lonnie reaches into my closet. "No!" I sputter. "Don't hide them there." I close the door super quick.

"What are you keeping back there? The *Millennium Falcon*?" He laughs. So do I, but my laughter comes out all choked up.

"It's just a bunch of The Destructor's dirty clothes," I say, which is more like an exaggeration than a lie.

When we're done hiding the eggs, Viva looks. It doesn't take her long to find all twenty-four eggs. Then Viva and I hide them for Lonnie.

Lonnie tries to look in the closet, but again I stop him. "We didn't put any in there." He moves on until he only has one egg left to find.

He's under The Destructor's bed. "Here it is!" He pulls it out.

"That's twenty-four!" Viva says.

"Wait!" Lonnie says, squeezing under the bed again. "There's one more." He reaches way in the back, and passes the last egg to me.

"Strange," Viva says. "That would make twenty-*five* eggs."

"Twenty-five?" I say. And that's when it cracks all over me.

The stench hits us before we have a chance to move. And by the time we get downstairs, it has consumed everything in its path. Viva's parents are already on their feet, and Lonnie's are right behind them.

Mom breathes deeply and then says to The Destructor, "Do you know anything about an egg under your bed?"

"Sure," he says. "I saved it from last year. It's my good-luck egg."

Needless to say, that egg was far from good luck, Easter supper was canceled, and I have to take another shower.

## APRIL FOOLS' DAY STRIKES AGAIN

I'm coming out of my third cleaning of the day. Dad is downstairs putting away the leftovers.

"Want a cookie?" he asks.

I nod. Sometimes Dad knows just what I need. I sit down and he brings me an Oreo and a glass of milk.

The Destructor sidles up next to me. "I'm sorry, Teddy." I turn my back to him. He comes around to my other side. "I said I'm sorry." I turn the other way. I don't want to have anything to do with The Destructor, but he comes around again. "HEY, TEDDY!" he screams in my ear. "CAN'T YOU HEAR ME?"

Dad says, "Time for bed, Jake," and scoops

The Destructor up before he can run away.

The Destructor screams, "But I said I was sorry!"

I don't hear what Dad answers and I don't care.

I take a bite of the cookie. "Blech!" April Fools' Day strikes again.

## IN IT TO WIN IT

Going back to school after a long weekend is usually hard, but because of the inventors' fair, it's pretty exciting.

Ms. Raffeli stands in front of the class. "There are only four days until the inventors' fair!" she says. "We want to be sure your inventions work, your posters are complete, and you know what you will do for your presentations."

Lewis is working on the note cards for our presentation, and Ny and Cornelio are coloring our poster. I'm looking at all the recycled stuff we have in the class to see if anything will help push the poo out. It's clear that I'm the only person in my group who's interested in making this work. I know it's not the invention part, but it seems so important.

At least Ms. Raffeli understands. "As Thomas Edison said, 'Our greatest weakness lies in giving up.'" Then she says, "Or as I like to say: we're *in it* to *win it*!"

I've never actually heard her say this, and it seems kind of corny, but I let it go because I actually feel the same.

## GRAN'S ADVICE PART 2

Mom is *still* working on the downstairs bathroom. Gran decided to go home early, because one bathroom with this many people was just too much for her. She left a note on my pillow that said: *Always remember, it's not important whether you win or lose, it's how you play the game.*

I have no idea why she wrote this to me, and I can't help wondering if it was meant for someone else, like my sisters, or The Destructor, or Mom and Dad, who can't even help each other.

Because the closet is bursting with plastic bags, I switch to my bureau. I stuff them under my pants and in my sweaters. Under my bed is next.

Hiding all these bags is really hard, not only because it's shocking how many plastic bags people use and throw away, but because every bag is a reminder that I'm not helping my friends.

Then I remember what Gran wrote, about how you play the game being the important thing. My friends are playing the game really badly. All they want is to beat each other, and they don't care how they do it.

After I think about it that way, I feel okay about what I'm doing. And it turns out Gran's advice has actually helped me, again!

## NO SUCH THING AS PRIVACY

Sharon won't get out of the bathroom. She's singing at the top of her lungs, and when I pound on the door, she yells, "You're not the only one in this family, Teddy!" and keeps on singing.

I am left with no other option.

So I go outside behind a tree in my backyard. The only place I know where there's a little privacy. But right then The Destructor and Grumpy Pigeon Man come outside with the pigeons. The pigeons fly up and around.

"Teddy!" The Destructor shouts. "Hi!" He waves at me.

"Is there no such thing as privacy?" I holler.

"You want to come over?" The Destructor shouts back.

Grumpy Pigeon Man says, "Don't take your eyes off

the birds, Pigeon Boy! Your brother has better things to do than help us."

I zip my fly and walk back inside the house. I want to be as far away from those two as I'd want to be from a Tunisian scorpion (the most venomous scorpion in the world).

Which, now that I think about it, has a lot in common with Grumpy Pigeon Man.

## LONGEST CAT FANGS

Three days and counting until the inventors' fair, and I still don't know how I'll get the poo out.

Lewis's eyes are all scrunched up and he's looking really serious. I think maybe he's thinking about the poo problem too. But when I ask him, he shakes his head and says, "Does Lonnie and Viva's ball look bigger than ours?"

Ny says, "Did you give them more bags, Teddy?"

"Well?" Cornelio says.

"No," I say; how can they even think that?

Lewis says, "You can't blame us for wondering. They are your best friends."

I think about that, and how right now they feel about as much like my best friends as an *Eusmilus* would. Strange but true, an *Eusmilus* is something like a saber-toothed cat that lived between thirty-seven and twenty-nine million years ago and holds the record for longest cat fangs (6 inches long). At lunch Lonnie, Viva, Max, and Angus corner me. I can definitely see their fangs.

"Did you give their group bags?" Viva asks.

Lonnie says, "Their ball is looking bigger."

I can't believe I'm having this conversation again. I give them the same answer I gave Lewis, Ny, and Cornelio and go back to thinking about poo, which, although it's gross, is a lot less dangerous.

## THE ANSWER

It's not until I'm back at home and eating my snack that I discover the answer I've been looking for. And it's all thanks to The Destuctor because for once he's not outside with the pigeons, but is inside playing with the play-dough pasta-making set that Gran gave him. He's making loads of pasta. He puts the play dough in, presses down, and out comes the pasta. It's not what I thought I'd use, but it's a perfect poo crank. Although technically it's not a crank, it's more of a pump.

That afternoon when he goes out to feed the pigeons, I slip the set into my backpack. When he comes back, he starts bawling about his missing pasta set, but Dad is too busy with dinner, and Mom is working on the bathroom. And for once I'm glad my parents are so distracted and not helping each other, or else they might actually look in my backpack and that would ruin everything!

## TWO DAYS AND COUNTING

Ms. Raffeli doesn't stop moving. She paces back and forth like she's part of the largest collection of windup toys (1,042).

"Two days until the inventors' fair!" Ms. Raffeli says. "Two days!" She wanders around the classroom, checking on each group, making sure all the inventions work.

"Three days until we break a world record," Ny whispers.

"That's what I was going to say!" Lewis says.

I'm too focused on our invention to think

about the world record. I've cut two holes in the dog. One is on the side, so the play-dough pasta kit can fit inside the dog. This hole is big enough for a hand to reach in and pump. The other hole is small and is in the back of the dog. This is where the poo will drop out after it's been squeezed through. I place one of my frozen chocolate pudding poos in the top and press down.

My heart is beating faster than usual. I've been struggling with this for so long. My group is finally paying attention to something besides breaking a world record. I press down harder. The frozen chocolate pudding pushes through the pasta kit, squeezes out the small hole in the back of the dog, and drops into the bag. As it falls, the weight of the poo slides the bag down

the track and away from the dog!

"It works! It works!" I shout, jumping up and down.

Lonnie and Viva look over.

"The poo worked," I say, explaining why I screamed. They scowl.

Lewis sighs. "I was going to bring in something just like that, but my dad said I couldn't."

There are a lot of hard records in *The Guinness Book of World Records*. For example, the fastest time to duct tape a person to a wall (28.53 seconds), the largest Jell-O mosaic (42 feet by 65 feet), and the youngest person to ski to the South Pole (16 years 190 days).

Really, if they can all do those things, you'd think Lewis could stop saying that he was going to say that too.

But I guess he can't, and I'm so happy right now I don't even care.

★ **MY TO-DO LIST (I CAN'T REMEMBER WHAT NUMBER I'M ON)** ★

1. Win the inventors' fair (only one day to go).
2. Survive the world record breakers (only two days to go).

## WINNER

The next day at school, all we do is practice our invention presentations in front of each other.

Ms. Raffeli doesn't say much because she's so busy chewing her nails, even though all the inventions look really good.

Lonnie and Viva's team have decided to call their invention the Battery-Operated Trash Masher, or BOTM. Lonnie connects a wire to a battery, which makes the motor move the masher up and down. Viva puts a paper cup under the masher and it is smooshed flat as a pancake.

The team with the musical baby blanket goes next. Jasmine B. holds the blanket while Jasmine H. holds a remote control. Jasmine B. pretends to cry like a baby until Jasmine H. presses a button and music starts to play. I have to say, it's very soothing, except for Angus, who's so nervous he's hopping around. That is not soothing.

The Go Kid Go Wagon team has revamped the crank so it goes farther than ever before.

And our group shows off how the poo squeezes out.

At the end of the day Ms. Raffeli says, "Get a good night's rest. Tomorrow, we show the school what winners you are!"

Strange but true, Alain Robert must have felt like a real winner after breaking the record for climbing to the top of the tallest building in the world (2,716 feet) and surviving. I feel the same about the Doggy-Doo Collector.

I'm sure I'm going to be the winner.

## CAUGHT

I'm eating a snack when Caitlin and Casey get home. They don't even say hi. They just weigh their trash, hand me all the plastic bags, and walk away bickering. I go upstairs and shove the bags under my bed.

When I stand up, The Destructor is staring straight at me.

Strange but true, the record for most knives thrown at a person in one minute is 102. The guy who did it practiced for five years before throwing the first knife at a human being.

The Destructor looks at me as if he'd like to break that record on me. Except without any practice.

"I'm saving this stuff for Lonnie and Viva." Once again I lie. "It's a surprise." Then I walk away as fast as I can, because it turns out lying to The Destructor makes me feel lousy.

## SABOTAGE

I'm downstairs reading the book Gran gave me when Mom yells, "It's done! It's done!" She's practically dancing across the room. "Try it out," she says. This seems like a ridiculous thing to ask, but because only The Destructor and I are home right now and she's pushing me into the bathroom, I don't have a choice.

I do my business and flush the toilet.

I can't believe what I see happening. The toilet is not flushing. Instead of the water going down like it's supposed to, it goes up and up and up until it falls over the sides. I push open the door, and again I can't believe what is happening.

The door is stuck. I thought she fixed this? "Mom!" I yell. "Mom!" She doesn't come to help.

It doesn't matter, though, because my sneakers are already covered in pee water—again!

I push once more and the door opens. The Destructor stares at me from the other side.

"Teddy?" Mom shows up.

"The door was stuck."

"It couldn't be." She opens and closes the door. It doesn't stick at all.

I look at The Destructor. I don't know what he did, but he's behind this. I know he is.

"What's all the water on the floor?" Mom asks.

"The toilet overflowed."

"Oh, phooey!"

She goes to grab the mop, and while she's gone, The Destructor hisses, "I'm watching you!"

I storm out of the room. I'll have to do something, because there's one thing for certain: The Destructor is not going to destroy me *not* helping my friends break a record. And even though that's one of the most confusing things I've ever thought, there's no time for me to think about it, because there's real work to be done.

## MOVING THE EVIDENCE

When The Destructor finally leaves to feed the pigeons, I race up to my room and wait until I see him in the aviary. That's when I make my move. Mom is back in the bathroom fixing the toilet again.

I creep around my room collecting all the bags I've hidden. I have three large garbage bags to stuff them all in. I have a plan.

I sneak down the hall with all the bags, then downstairs and into the basement.

The back of the basement is dark and gross.

I push past cobwebs and weird shadows until I'm in the farthest corner of the basement. The corner no one goes in. I hide the bags behind an old trunk, where they will never be found.

I run up the stairs as fast as I can, because it's so creepy down there, it really does give me the willies.

I might know how to outsmart a little brother, but a ghost? I'm not so sure.

## MORE NERVOUS THAN I REALIZED

"It's the big day!" Ms. Raffeli says. "We've done everything we can, and I'm proud of each and every one of you!" She explains how each class in the grade goes down one at a time to set up their projects. Because she's obviously so nervous, she tells us for the third time how the voting works. How each student votes on the invention they like the most, how Principal Johnson tallies the votes, and how the project with the most votes wins.

We finally head down to the cafeteria to set up our projects. Kids from the other two fourth-grade classes are already there. Each invention has a table, and the room is split in half so students can still eat lunch while the inventors' fair goes on. There are so many different projects, it boggles my mind.

Strange but true, the record for most nails hammered into a piece of wood in one minute is 24. My heart is pounding faster than the hammer that broke that record. And I can honestly say, it's fast.

## INVENTORS' FAIR:
## THINGS I WASN'T PREPARED FOR

1. How scary it is to have a schoolful of students walking through and looking at what you've made.
2. How easy they think it is to make an invention and how they enjoy telling us what they would do differently.

3. How funny squeezing poo out of a fake dog is. No matter how many times you do it, it's always hilarious. And especially when it makes a farting noise for no reason that we can explain.

## INVENTORS' FAIR: THINGS I WASN'T PREPARED FOR PART 2

There are a lot of amazing inventions. My favorites are:

1. The Ping-Pong Ball Shooter, which keeps shooting balls across the room so you can play even when you're by yourself.
2. The Wave Creator, to make it more exciting for a fish in its bowl—I don't know how the fish actually feels about this, but it makes me feel seasick just thinking about it.

3. The Deaf Cat Caller gets the attention of a deaf cat! I didn't even know there were deaf cats, but between the catnip,

the laser pointer, and the fuzzy balls, it must work. It definitely works on everyone here.

As much as I like all these, I'm still confident we will win. I mean, really, how could we lose with a poo catcher?

## INVENTORS' FAIR: THINGS I WASN'T PREPARED FOR PART 3

1. We have to stay here all day. My feet are killing me.
2. It's a super-hot day, and the cafeteria is the worst place to be on a hot day. It makes you feel like you're being baked for lunch.
3. Parents show up asking lots of serious questions, like, "How is this an invention?" Why do they ask stuff like that?

## SHE DIDN'T!

Viva's mom is one of the first parents to arrive. She wanders around asking loads of questions.

Lonnie's mom and dad both come. Lewis sees his mom and dad holding hands when they walk in. "Ew!" he says. "They're so gross." They might be gross, but they're not at all the way he described. From his description I thought they'd be fighting the whole time.

Then Mom walks in! I can't believe it. She never comes to school events. She's usually got her hands full with The Destructor, and I'm just wondering how she got rid of him, when a wing pokes out from behind her. "Oh no!" I say. "She didn't!"

Lewis looks at me. "She didn't what?"

Then a pigeon head sticks out. "Oh," I say. "She did!"

"She did what?" Cornelio asks.

"How could she?" I say. "Doesn't she know what he'll do?"

"What who will do?" Ny says.

I turn to my group and say, "Guard the invention. My brother is here."

Mom comes over; she's holding The Destructor by the hand, but he's tugging to get away. I watch The Destructor flap over to Lonnie and Viva. Mom introduces herself to my group and admires our invention.

"How do you get the poo to come out?" she asks.

Ny says, "That was Teddy's idea. He brought in a play-dough kit."

I go red in the face as Mom says, "Really? Is it by any chance the pasta-making one?"

"That's right," Cornelio says. "It works really well. Want to try it?"

I know I should explain, but I can't take my eyes off Lonnie, Viva, and The Destructor, who look over at me. The Destructor smiles.

And it's not a nice smile.


## AND IF THAT WASN'T ENOUGH

Ms. Raffeli comes over and says, "Things are looking really good!" She sounds almost giddy. "You're getting a lot of votes!" And she trots off to the help Go Kid Go Wagon team, who has gotten jammed under a lunch table.

I can't describe how good I feel right now. It almost takes my mind off what The Destructor was up to with Lonnie and Viva.

Mom and The Destructor wander back over. Lewis is demonstrating our invention for a bunch of fourth graders, while Mom tells me how proud

she is of me, even if we will be talking about the stolen pasta kit later.

Just then I hear a kid screech, "He ate the poo!"

And another kid yells, "Gross!"

I turn around in time to see The Destructor shoving the poo into his mouth.

"Jake!" Mom shouts. But it's too late. He eats all our poo.

"I love that stuff!" The Destructor says as Mom pulls him away.

Strange but true, the loudest animal sound comes from blue whales and fin whales, the loudest insect is the African cicada, and the loudest land animal is the male howler monkey.

I don't care how loud those are, if I weren't in the middle of the inventors' fair, I'd scream louder than all of them, because The Destructor just struck again.

## INVENTORS' FAIR: THINGS I WASN'T PREPARED FOR PART 4

1. The Destructor eating our poo.
2. Not having any poo means no more demonstrations, and there are two more grades still to come through.
3. The disappointed looks of those two grades when we tell them we're out of poo.
4. Lonnie and Viva glaring at me for the rest of the inventors' fair.
5. That I'm actually glad that the inventors' fair is over.

## FREE TIME

We're back in the classroom and Ms. Raffeli says, "Well, now all we can do is wait."

She gives us free time for the rest of the day, which sounds better than it actually is, because there's only a half an hour left to the school day. On top of that, I can't stop thinking about how we'll lose the inventors' fair because The

Destructor ate all our poo, but no one wants to talk about that. All they can talk about is the plastic bag record. Everyone, that is, except Lonnie and Viva, who are not talking to me at all. I have a pretty good idea what The Destructor said to them, but I am not saying a thing until they do.

If Lonnie and Viva were really Jedis, they would talk to me. But they aren't, which means they believe him or they've joined the dark side.

Either way, there's no saving them. And for this first time in my life I can't wait for free time to be over.


## LOSING MY APPETITE

I'm downstairs in the kitchen having a snack. Mom and Dad come out of the bathroom together. I guess Mom decided to ask for help with the toilet.

"You did it perfectly," Dad says. "You can't help it if a ball of play dough got stuck down there. It happened with a sock before."

"Gee!" I say. "I wonder who did that?"

They don't answer me because they're kissing. After all their fighting, this is a real surprise.

Just then, Sharon stomps in. "Well, that's it. The little beast is obviously not going to get sick and the play is tonight, which means I'm going to be a dumb orphan, while she has her moment to shine."

"Don't worry," Mom says. "We'll all be there rooting for you, even if you are only a dumb orphan."

"That's exactly what I don't want," Sharon says, and huffs off. I hear the upstairs bathroom door slam.

For once Sharon and I are in agreement. I don't want to go to her play either. After the day I've had, just thinking about it makes me feel sick to my stomach.

Mom turns to Dad. "Can I help you with dinner tonight?"

"I cannot tell you," Dad says, "how much I would like that."

I watch as they pull out pots and pans and start cooking together.

I'd like to tell them how much I like this, because finally we'll have something edible to eat, but they're being so lovey-dovey that I actually lose my appetite. I have to leave the room; it's the only way I think I might get hungry again.

## I'M NOT GOING TO ENJOY IT

After dinner, which was really delicious, even though my parents are gross, I climb into bed. There isn't anywhere else that I want to be. I can't get over the fact that I really had a chance at winning the inventors' fair, and my brother messed it up.

There's a knock on the door, and Dad says, "Time to go."

"I don't want to go," I say.

Dad says, "We're going."

"Why should I go?"

"Because we're a family."

"You and Mom have not been acting like a family."

He looks confused, so I explain. "You've been fighting for weeks over who's doing what job, and suddenly tonight you're nice to each other, and we're all supposed to be a happy family? Well, I don't feel like it."

Dad is real quiet. "We're going to your sister's play."

I can tell by his voice that he means it. So I get out of bed.

"I'm not going to enjoy it," I say.

"You don't have to," he says. "Life is not

always fun. Sometimes we just have to show up and somehow that it makes it all better."

## THE PLAY

Lonnie and Viva arrive together. I scrunch down low in my seat so they can't see me.

Mom says, "Teddy, there's Lonnie and Viva. Don't you want to sit with them?"

I scrunch down lower.

"I don't know what is going on with the three of you," Mom says, "but I hope you sort it out."

I don't say anything to Mom, but I don't know how we'll sort it out. And it's all The Destructor's fault.

Finally the lights dim and the show starts. I hate to say it, I didn't think it would be a great night, but in the end I had a good time—a really good time. Sharon is a real star, even if she's not Annie.

In fact, I wouldn't want to be Annie. It's easy to stand out when you play the part of the main kid. But Sharon played one of the sad orphans left behind when Annie goes off to the mansion, and she did a good job. I totally believed she was an orphan and not my sister. I really felt bad for her, stuck at that orphanage with the horrible Miss Hannigan.

We're about to leave the theater, but Grace dashes off. "I want an interview," she yells. A few minutes later we see her talking to Sharon. Sharon is smiling her face off. So is Grace.

Jerome walks past them. He stops and looks at Sharon like he's got something to say, and then turns away.

But that's when Sharon shouts, "Hey! Jerome!" She motions for him to come over, and he does, and Grace interviews him, too. And then—this part I wouldn't believe if I hadn't seen it with my own eyes—but Sharon pulls over the girl who played Annie and introduces her to Grace. Then Sharon grabs Jerome and they walk away arm in arm, leaving Grace talking to the Annie girl.

For about a second I feel really happy. Then I see Lonnie and Viva. Strange but true, the most venomous jellyfish in the world is the box jellyfish, also known as Flecker's sea wasp. And even though I know Lonnie and Viva and I aren't friends anymore, when they walk straight past me and don't say anything, it hurts as much as if I were stung by that jellyfish.

## CLOSE THE DOOR

The next morning I wake up so early it's still dark outside. I don't feel good at all. It's not the kind of not good that comes from eating the most powdered doughnuts in three minutes (6). It's the kind of not good that would come from parachuting out of a rocket 127,852 feet above Earth like Felix Baumgartner did. It's the kind of not good feeling that makes me feel antsy, and twitchy, and not able to stay in bed.

The Destructor is snoring. I look at the clock. I've got an hour until he'll wake up. I sneak out of bed, grab some clothes, and go to the aviary. I don't know why I do this, but I figure I can slip in, hang out a little with the pigeons, and be gone before either Grumpy Pigeon Man or The Destructor arrives. I miss the pigeons.

It feels like forever since I've been out here. I turn over a bucket and sit listening to the quiet sounds the pigeons make, fluffing and cooing. It's cozy and warm. It would be good to be a pigeon.

The sun starts coming into the aviary. I'm surprised The Destructor hasn't shown up yet. I think about leaving, but I can't. It's like I'm glued to my spot, which has a lot to do with the fact that Obi-Wan Kenobi, Stass Allie, Yoda, and Ima-Gun Di are all sitting on me. I can't think of the last time I felt this happy.

Then The Destructor crashes in. He stands in the doorway. "What did you do with them?" he asks.

"Close the door!" I say.

He doesn't move. "The plastic bags?" he says. "What did you do with them?"

"None of your business."

"You never want to share anything!" The Destructor hollers.

"What's that supposed to mean?"

He's still standing in the door, like he can't decide if he's coming in or going out.

"Exactly what it means. You don't share."

And as I stand there taking in what he's just said, Admiral Ackbar flies up to The Destructor and straight out the door. Princess Leia, Jar Jar Binks, C-3PO, and Paploo follow, swooping past The Destructor like starfighters. The Destructor is frozen, unable to move even as the four Jedi pigeons swoop out, beating their wings against his face.

"Close the door!" I shout, but with all the flapping, he can't do anything except cover his face with his own wing as more and more pigeons slip out, following Admiral Ackbar to freedom.

I run to the door and watch as they fly higher.

The Destructor cries, "I don't have my slingshot!"


## HAWK

We watch as the pigeons fly around, silenced by what just happened and not able to do a thing. The Destructor's eyes dart around the sky, and then he points. I'm about to get Grumpy Pigeon Man when The Destructor hollers, "There! There it is!"

I look up. The Destructor is right. A hawk circles above the pigeons.

"Do something!" he yells.

"Do something?" I say. "What can I do?" I

look around, trying to find some way to warn the pigeons, to call them back home. I don't have a slingshot, and even if I did, I couldn't hit a hawk with it.

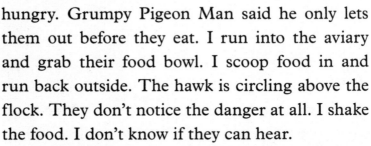

And then I think of it. Food! The pigeons haven't eaten yet and must be hungry. Grumpy Pigeon Man said he only lets them out before they eat. I run into the aviary and grab their food bowl. I scoop food in and run back outside. The hawk is circling above the flock. They don't notice the danger at all. I shake the food. I don't know if they can hear.

I shake the food again, rattling it more and more. The hawk circles closer and closer, then it dives. I shake the food harder. The pigeons swerve sharply down, careening toward me. "Hold the door open," I yell at The Destructor, who pulls it open and stands out of the way as a cascade of birds flies into the aviary. The Destructor slams the door closed to keep them in.

Three pigeons are still out. Paploo, C-3PO, and Admiral Ackbar. I fling food on the ground. "Land," I beg. "Come on and land."

The hawk is diving again. Going for Paploo. The hawk's talons are out, about to grab the bird, but at the last minute, Admiral Ackbar dives at it, attacking the hawk, distracting it. I shake the food more. C-3PO guides Paploo down as the hawk and Admiral Ackbar twist and turn in the sky. They're caught in each other's feet and wings. Admiral Ackbar beats his wings. The hawk loses its grip and drops Admiral Ackbar. The hawk rights itself, then attacks again, but Admiral Ackbar is ready. He flings himself at the hawk, driving the hawk away with his wings, and feet, and beak. Finally the hawk turns sharply and flies off. Admiral Ackbar flaps

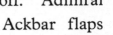

down and collapses at my feet.

"He's bleeding," I say as I scoop him up in my hands. "Get Grump—Mr. Marney. Quick!"

The Destructor runs to Grumpy Pigeon Man's house and bangs on his door.

Mr. Marney comes out, rubbing his eyes. "For the love of pigeon food, what's going on?!" he hollers.

The Destructor pulls him over to me, his eyes full of tears. "Hawk," he squeaks.

## SHARING

The Destructor is so upset we call Mom, who comes and takes him home. Grumpy Pigeon Man and I stay in the aviary with Admiral Ackbar.

Grumpy Pigeon Man passes Admiral Ackbar to me. "Gentle, he's not a bag of frozen peas," he grumps, as if I was being anything but gentle. I'm so scared I'll hurt him that I'm being more careful than if I was touching the tallest homegrown cactus (78.8 feet).

He takes out the pigeons' first aid kit, grabs a bottle, and dumps some liquid from it on a cotton ball. He carefully wipes Admiral Ackbar's cuts. Next he pulls out a drinking straw, cuts the straw in half, and makes a slit down the middle. "Hold out the hurt leg," he says. He slips the straw onto Admiral Ackbar's leg like a cast, then grabs some bandages and wraps them around the cast. He places a hot-water bottle wrapped in towels in a box. "Put him in here," Mr. Marney says. "Careful!"

"I am being careful!" I snap. Grumpy Pigeon Man ignores me. "What's going to happen to him?" I ask more quietly.

"He needs rest and warmth. He'll live in the house for a while, where I can keep an eye on him." Grumpy Pigeon Man adjusts the towels. "I've seen worse."

"He was so brave," I say. "If it wasn't for him, I don't know what would have happened."

Grumpy Pigeon Man pets Admiral Ackbar.

"It's not my fau—" I start to say, but I stop.

"What were you doing here? You said you quit."

"I know that's what you want."

He looks at me. "Where'd you get that idea?"

"All the time you spend with The Destructor. How you let him do everything. Come here whenever he wants."

Grumpy Pigeon Man shakes his head and

sighs. "Tent Boy, I hired you to take care of these birds. I know you love them. But you don't get to be the only one. That would  be like inventing electricity and never sharing it. It's a bad way to live."

I think about this. I think about how Edison and Tesla fought over electricity. How my family fights over a million things. How my friends fight over a world record. How I fight with The Destructor, my family, my friends, even Grumpy Pigeon Man. Then I say, "Sharing isn't easy."

"I know, but the more you do it, the easier it is." He pauses. "Or, at least, that's what people tell me."

And then I figure something out and I say, "You have to share me too."

"What's that mean?"

"I like taking care of your pigeons, but I also like breaking records."

He sighs. "Sharing isn't easy."

"I know, but the more you do it, the easier it is." I pause. "At least, that's what one of the smartest people I know tells me."

Grumpy Pigeon Man smiles and so do I.

## MOST SUCCINCT WORD

What Grumpy Pigeon Man says reminds me of a record I've never really understood. It's the record for most succinct word in the world. I know *succinct* means short and to the point, because it was a vocabulary word once. But the most succinct word in the world comes from a language spoken only in the tip of Argentina and Chile. The word is *mamihlapinatapai*. It doesn't seem succinct when you look at all those letters, but it turns out its meaning is very precise. It means to do something for someone else even though you don't want to.

And suddenly I stand up. "I've got to go," I say.

Grumpy Pigeon Man frowns.

"I've made a terrible mistake."

"Only one?" Grumpy Pigeon Man laughs. "Then you're doing better than the rest of us." He picks up the box and heads out the door with me. "Will I see you later?"

"You can't get rid of me, even if you try."

I dash away, because I finally know what I have to do, and it's totally different from Gran's advice.

## MOST DANGEROUS SHARK

"Mom," I yell as I walk into the house. "Mom! I need help! Can you drive me to school?"

Mom says, "That's not a problem. We're leaving in a minute; Maggie has her track meet there today."

Just then Caitlin and Casey run down the stairs. They're dressed all in green clothes and their faces are painted up like the earth.

"What are you doing?" I ask.

"Earth Day celebration," they say.

"What's Earth Day?"

They look at me like I'm asking who the tallest man ever was (Robert Wadlow—8 feet 11.1 inches). Everyone knows that guy. After they recover from their shock they explain that it's the day where people come together to celebrate taking care of the earth; they do things to show that they want to keep it clean and safe, and bring attention to ways we all can help.

Caitlin says, "It was actually a few days ago."

Casey says, "But today there's a big celebration over at your school."

They both say, "Didn't you see the posters?"

"Clearly, I didn't see the posters, because if I had seen the posters, I would know there was an

Earth Day celebration."

"You should start thinking about other stuff besides yourself!" Caitlin says.

"She's right," Casey says. They hop on their bikes and take off.

"That's what I'm trying to do!" I run down into the basement. I creep past the cobwebs and shadows, and pull out the bags of plastic bags I've been hoarding. I don't know what exactly I'm going to do once I get to school, but like Dad said, showing up is the important thing.

We all pile into the car. Luckily Caitlin and Casey biked, or there wouldn't be room for the bags.

Grace turns around. "What's all that stuff?"

"Maybe a new story," I say.

"I don't think so!" Grace stomps on my foot. That girl has long legs and a powerful foot. But I've got bigger things to worry about than whether my toes are broken.

The Destructor stares out the window. It's better this way.

The parking lot at school is packed. The place is swarming with people. There are track things set up all over the place.

"I'm out of here." Maggie leaps out of the car

and runs off to meet her team.

And because of the Earth Day celebration, there are banners asking people to conserve water, to recycle, to plant more trees, to turn off lights, and even to use fewer plastic bags. It's really amazing.

"Oh, there's Jerome!" Sharon says. "See you later."

"I can't believe I'm saying this, but I'm going to interview the track teams," Grace says, and takes off across the field.

Caitlin and Casey bike up.

"Beat you!" Caitlin yells.

"It's a tie," Casey says. "We rode up at exactly the same time!"

I leave the bags in the car and walk closer to the school.

That's when I see the plastic bag balls. They are right by the swings. Lonnie, Viva, Max, and Angus stand in front of one. Lewis, Ny, Cornelio, and Serena are in front of the other one. I run over.

They all see me at the same time. And they look at me like I'm the white shark—the record holder for most dangerous shark in the world. It makes me stop in my tracks, but then I remember I'm not the white shark, I'm just Teddy, and I walk up closer.

## RECORD BREAKER VS. RECORD BREAKER

"Oh brother!" Viva says. "I told you he would come!"

Lonnie says, "If you're going to beat us all, get it over with."

My throat tightens. "Do you really think I'd do that?" I ask.

Lonnie says, "Stop pretending. Jake told us everything."

"You're here to compete against us," Viva says. "You want to break another record on your own."

Lonnie shakes his head. "You should have just told us the truth."

I look at Lonnie and Viva. How can they believe this?

And just then Ms. Raffeli's voice rings out. "Would one of you please tell me what is actually going on with these bags?"

## ME AND THE BAGS

By this time, just about everyone I know is standing around us. There's Ms. Raffeli, most of my class, all my sisters except Maggie, my parents, Jerome, and of course The Destructor.

Mom is saying, "Jake? Did you tell Lonnie and Viva that?"

Dad says, "Teddy, what's going on?"

Every kid is also talking at the same time, until Ms. Raffeli claps her hands and we all get silent.

Mom says, "I wish I could do that."

Ms. Raffeli's eyebrows go up and Mom stops talking.

"So you're telling me," Ms. Raffeli says, "that you have all been trying to break a record in my classroom and I didn't know about it?"

We nod.

"I thought it was for the inventors' fair."

We nod.

"And I presume," she carries on, "that at first it was for the largest collection of plastic bags."

We nod again.

"And then," she says, "you all started to fight and your group split up."

I have to say, if Ms. Raffeli ever retires from teaching, she should become a detective because she knows a lot more than I would ever think she would.

She looks at me. "The only thing I don't understand is, why is everyone mad at you?"

That's when all of us start talking at the same time.

"Teddy wanted his own record."

"He didn't even tell us!"

"He didn't want anyone else to win."

Ms. Raffeli claps her hands again. "One at a time," she says. Then she looks at Lonnie. He explains how at first I was helping, and then how after the group split up I stopped, and how I kept all my bags, and how I was trying to break the record all by myself, but no one knew that until The Destructor told them.

She looks at me. "Teddy?" she says. "Is this true?"

I take a deep breath and say, "I have been hiding them."

"See!" Viva erupts, but Ms. Raffeli stops her.

"Go on, Teddy."

"I didn't hide them to break a record."

I look up and see Jasmine B. and Jasmine H. off to the side. They smile at me and give me a thumbs-up.

"So why did you do it?" Lewis says. "I mean, whose side are you on?"

"I'm not on anyone's side." I look at Lonnie, Viva, and even Lewis. "I'm just tired of all the fighting."

Lonnie and Viva look at the two plastic bag balls. There's a silence that seems to last as long as the longest-burning lightbulb, which has been going since 1901!

And then Lonnie says, "In the words of Yoda: 'The fear of loss is a path to the dark side.' I think I wanted to win a little too much, but if I think about it, I'm tired of all the fighting too."

Viva says, "That's what I was going to say."

"Hey!" Lewis says. "That's what I say!" Then he raises his hand for a high five, and Lonnie and Viva and I raise ours, and so do Angus, and Ny, and Cornelio, and Max, and Serena. We do a high five, except with all those hands we miss and end up slapping each other instead.

And like the two Jasmines say, it's a big mess, but this mess is actually funny and makes us laugh.


## RECORD BREAKING DAY

Because we want to start all over again and really do it together this time, we unroll the two plastic bag balls. When they are totally unwound, we reattach them, one end to one end, and then start rolling them back together.

And even though it's a lot of work, it doesn't matter, because the people here for Earth Day get all excited and take pictures, and people who are at the track meet see how much fun we're having and they want to help, too. We keep a record of how many bags we have. We tie and roll and tie and roll. We add the ones I brought and even ones that people have here today. The ball gets bigger and bigger, until it's as wide as ten of us standing side by side and as tall as two of us. If we could stand on top of each other.

Grace is writing the whole thing down and says this story is going to be her big break. But just then a TV crew from Channel 7 appears. "I'll handle this," she screams at us. "You keep rolling!"

But Lewis walks over to the Channel 7 reporter and says, "It was all my idea!"

The Channel 7 reporter starts asking loads of questions until Ny, Serena, Max, and Angus interrupt and say a couple of kids came up with the idea, but the whole class worked on it together.

"That's what I was going to say!" Lewis says.

Ny shakes her head and crosses her arms.

"I was! I promise I was just getting to that!"

I go back to the ball and see The Destructor running around shouting at people to bring their plastic bags to us. Caitlin and Casey keep biking

away and then coming back with more used bags. Mom and Dad are holding hands and talking to Ms. Raffeli. And I have to admit, it is nice that Mom and Dad are getting along again, and it's not just nice because of the food.

That's when Maggie limps up behind them along with another girl. I leave the plastic bag ball for a second, which is fine because Jasmine B. and Jasmine H. are having a good time keeping us all organized.

"What happened?" I ask.

Lewis runs up behind me. "That's what I was going to ask."

I sigh.

"I mean it," he says. "That's my sister, Bella."

I look at the girl next to Maggie. "That's your sister?"

Maggie says, "Do you know Bella Colon?"

"Bella Colon is your sister?" I say.

"Yeah," he says. "So what."

I look over at Maggie and Bella, who are suddenly not rivals.

Maggie says, "We collided. We're both out of the competition with twisted ankles."

"After all that work?" I say.

She shrugs. "Training is the fun part." Bella and Maggie limp off to watch the races.

I nod. I know what she's talking about because, strange but true, breaking a record is not as fun as *trying* to break a record.

## STRANGEST THINGS TO FALL OUT OF THE SKY

By the end of the track meet we've rolled and counted eighteen thousand bags! We have lots of photos to send to the world record people. Channel 7 interviewed us, and because it was the Earth Day celebration, Lonnie talked about how our record shows people that we need to use fewer plastic bags! And that part was especially cool, because even though we didn't plan it, our record became something more than just a record.

And now Lonnie, Viva, and I are sitting in the grass. I could tell them a million times how sorry I am that I didn't tell them the truth, but I think we all feel sorry for something, so we don't need to say it.

Strange but true, there are a lot things I don't understand in this world; for example, there's a list in *The Guinness Book of World Records* of the strangest things to fall out of the sky: electric rain, birds' blood, green rain, nails, blue rain, a tortoise in a hailstone, frogs, pwdre ser (also known as star rot), silver coins, and something called angel hair. Like I said, I don't understand this list at all; I have no idea what most of those things are. But the list proves that the world is stranger than I ever could know, and if that's true, then anything is possible.

Like breaking world records, or sharing the aviary, or even becoming friends again with your friends.

## GOOD NEWS AND BAD NEWS

Two days later, we're back at school. It's lunch, and Lonnie, Viva, and I sit at our old table. Ny joins us, and Angus, and Cornelio, and Serena, and Max. Principal Johnson is going to announce the winner of the inventors' fair after lunch.

Lewis walks over and says, "Is there room for me?"

"Sure," Lonnie and Viva say at the same time.

And I admit, it feels like we're all one group again. Maybe even a group that could break a record for the largest game of leapfrog (1,348 people) or largest simultaneous jump (569,069 people) or even the largest tea party (32,681 people), except I don't think I like tea.

As Lewis settles in, he says, "I've got some good news and some bad news, guys."

"What's the bad news?" Viva asks.

"I was doing a little research about the bags and discovered that a school in California broke our record. They had 36,700 plastic bags."

Viva's jaw drops. "That means we need—"

"Another 18,701 plastic bags to break the record!" Lewis interrupts.

"That's what I was going to say," Viva says.

"I'm so sorry," I say. "I know how much you

wanted to break the record."

"Who cares," he says. "Did you see the paper today?"

"No," I say.

"We're all over it. And on top of that, I've already been asked for a TV interview."

"So is that the good news?" Lonnie asks.

"No way." Lewis smiles. "The good news is we get to keep on trying to break our record! I couldn't think of anything cooler!"

I laugh. "That's what I call a win-win situation!"

At the end of recess, Ms. Raffeli surprises us with an ice cream party. "You all deserve this because you've worked so hard together. Really, whether we win or lose today, you're all winners."

Then Angus falls on his knees and says, "Can we have pajama day next week?"

Ms. Raffeli's eyebrows fly up. "Don't push it, Angus."

"How about crazy hair day?"

"Angus!"

It's really nice to see she hasn't changed too much.

We have to eat fast because Principal Johnson is waiting for our whole grade in the library to announce the winner.

"In third place," she says, "from Ms. Cleary's class: the Ping-Pong Ball Shooter." Everyone claps, and the kids who made that walk up to the front. "In second place, from Mr. Jenkins's class, the Foot Massager."

We all clap again. And really, it's surprisingly great to be happy for other people who are winning. Principal Johnson raises her hand for quiet. "And for first place, from Ms. Raffeli's class, the Battery Operated Trash Masher, or as they like to call it, the BOTM."

I look over at Ms. Raffeli and she's beaming, and before I know it I'm on my feet clapping like crazy, because I'm so proud of my friends, and even though I would have liked to win, it's all great, because actually, just like Ms. Raffeli said, I am already a winner.

I have my friends again, and I can tell you that that is way better than winning the inventors' fair.

## ★ MY TO-DO LIST NUMBER WHATEVER ★

I'd like to start a new list, but right now I don't have a single thing to put on it.

Maybe that's better.

## CAN BOY

I go around to the aviary. I thought The Destructor would be here, because I couldn't find him back at home, but he isn't. I hear the door open and figure that'll be him, but it's Grumpy Pigeon Man, carrying Admiral Ackbar. "He's a tough one," Grumpy Pigeon Man says. "But he still needs his friends."

There's a knock on the door. Lonnie and Viva walk in. Grumpy Pigeon Man never shows any emotion except grumpiness, but I can tell he's happy to see Lonnie and Viva, because he says, "It's about time you came over."

We all sit together and watch the pigeons flutter. We listen to their soft coos. Even Admiral Ackbar joins in.

Grumpy Pigeon Man says, "How's the world record going?"

"Breaking a record is lot harder than I thought," Viva says.

"We should try for another one," Lonnie says. "It'll be months before we break the plastic bag record."

"Got any ideas?" I ask.

Grumpy Pigeon Man says, "How about going the longest amount of time not breaking a record?"

And we all laugh because we know that will never happen.

"Anyone seen Jake?" Grumpy Pigeon Man asks.

"I thought he was here," I say.

Right then, The Destructor walks in. He's covered from head to toe in old tin cans and duct tape.

"Call me Can Boy!" he says. "I'm saving the world by recycling!"

The smell of the old food from the cans stinks up the aviary worse than any pigeon poo ever could, and the racket those cans make scares all the birds. They fly up and around the loft, and just as Paploo flies over my head, he poos right on me.

There are people who would get really bothered about getting pooed on. There are people who think it's the grossest thing ever, and others who would call me a loser because I got pooed on.

But after everything I've been through, trying to break records, making an invention, losing the aviary, and almost losing my friends, I know that getting pooed on is no big deal; it doesn't make me a winner or a loser, it just makes me dirty (and it *might* bring me good luck).

And strange but true, I'm fine with that.

# ACKNOWLEDGMENTS

1. **Fantastic family**—Sean, Adelaide, Georgia
2. **Stupendous sister**—Sarah
3. **Fabulous friends**—Near and far, you know who you are
4. **Awe-inspiring agent**—Tina Wexler
5. **Phenomenal publisher**—Katherine Tegen
6. **Exceptional editor**—Maria Barbo
7. **Oh-so-talented HarperCollins team**—Amy Ryan, Aurora Parlagreco, Bethany Reis, Mark Rifkin, Alana Whitman, Ro Romanello, Carmen Alvarez, Jean McGinley, Alpha Wong, Sarah Ought, Sheala Howley, Molly Motch, Patty Rosati, Kelsey Horton, Rebecca Schwarz.
8. **Illustrious illustrator**—Trevor Spencer
9. **Marvelous MFA**—Hamline University faculty and students

10. Tremendous teachers, librarians, and booksellers—You rock!
11. Remarkable record breakers—all the people who break records, and who try to break records, and *The Guinness Book of World Records* for keeping track of them all

## TEDDY'S REASONS TO RECYCLE

1. Saves space (less trash).
2. Saves air (less pollution).
3. Saves life (more of everything).

## TEDDY'S ADVICE FOR INVENTORS

1. Be curious.
2. Be imaginative.
3. Be collaborative.

## TEDDY'S TIP-TOP INVENTORS

1. Thomas Edison: holds patents for 2,332 inventions. (Shunpei Yamazaki holds even more!)
2. Nikola Tesla: invented a lot of cool stuff that we still use today, like X rays. (More important, he really liked pigeons!)
3. Lonnie G. Johnson: invented the Super Soaker. (This might be the best invention ever.)
4. Marie Van Brittan Brown: inventor of the home security system. (Could use one in my room.)
5. Garrett Morgan: inventor of the traffic signal. (We need one of these, specifically for the bathroom!)

## TEDDY'S TOP TEN PIGEON FUN FACTS

1. They're old: Pigeons have lived alongside humans for a really long time (at least since about 5,000 years ago).
2. They're sporty: Pigeons can fly for hundreds of miles in one day, some can do back flips, and they can even play ping pong!
3. They're fast: They can fly up to 100 miles per hour!
4. They're helpful: They carried messages for the ancient Greeks during the Olympics, for Genghis Khan, for armies during World War II, and even for regular people who couldn't get mail any other way.
5. They're smart: They have been taught to recognize the letters and numbers.
6. They're artistic: They have been used to take aerial photographs and can see more colors than humans can!

7.  They're adaptable: They can live any-where—except the North and South Pole.
8.  They're lifesavers: Pigeons have been used to find people lost at sea.
9.  They're loving: Both male and female pigeons sit on the eggs, and both feed their young.
10. They're adorable: No explanation needed.

# TOP THREE THINGS
# YOU WILL FIND IN BOOK THREE

1. World records
2. A dog in a diaper
3. Rules for surviving The Destructor!

When Teddy's great-aunt Ursula moves in, Teddy is not happy. She has rules about everything from juice to jumping rope and even record breaking! But Great-Aunt Ursula's newest rule—PIGEONS ARE NOT PETS—puts Grumpy Pigeon Man's pigeons in danger. And Teddy may have to bend a few rules to save them!

Teddy goes from record breaker to rule breaker in his hilarious and heartwarming quest to do what's right, even if it's a little bit wrong.

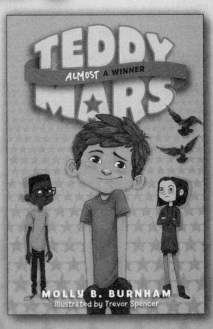